20
p

KU-350-926

The Mystery of
Cabin Island

THE MYSTERY OF CABIN ISLAND

The Hardy boys are elated over their good luck when wealthy Elroy Jefferson invites them to spend Christmas vacation at his private retreat on Cabin Island. But when Frank and Joe make a reconnaissance trip in their ice-yacht the *Seagull* to the island, a belligerent stranger orders them off. Why?

Before twenty-four hours have passed, the Hardys find themselves involved in two mysteries: the first concerns the recent disappearance of Mr Jefferson's grandson, Johnny; the second, the baffling theft of a priceless collection of antique medals which took place two years before. The young detectives, with their pals Chet Morton and Biff Hooper, pursue both cases on the icebound, snow-covered island.

Sabotage to the *Seagull*, danger to themselves, and a ghostly prowler do not daunt Frank and Joe in their search for Johnny Jefferson and for clues to the stolen antique medals. How the teenage investigators outwit a ruthless foe and succeed in solving both mysteries makes for mounting suspense in this fast-moving adventure.

Too late Joe flung himself sideways.

THE HARDY BOYS MYSTERY STORIES

THE MYSTERY OF CABIN ISLAND

By FRANKLIN W. DIXON

COLLINS · London & Glasgow

ISBN 0 00 160526 7
PRINTED AND MADE IN GREAT BRITAIN

CONTENTS

·1·

Threat on Cabin Island

"WHAT a reward!" Joe Hardy exclaimed. "You mean we can stay at Cabin Island over the winter vacation?"

"Right. Starting the day after Christmas," said Frank. "The whole place is ours, and Mr Jefferson says he'll throw another mystery our way."

"About what?"

"Wouldn't say. He'll tell us at his home tomorrow when we get the key."

The Hardy boys were elated over their good luck. The young detectives recently had broken a car theft ring, and in gratitude for the return of his automobile, Elroy Jefferson, a wealthy resident of Bayport, had made the offer of his private retreat near the entrance to Barmet Bay.

Impulsive, blond-haired Joe snapped his fingers. "Let's call Chet and Biff and take our ice-yacht over to the island. I'd like to give it a quick preview."

"Okay. We can meet 'em at our dock."

Dark-haired Frank, eighteen and a year older than Joe, was just as eager to set foot on Cabin Island and also to skim over the ice, now glossy smooth after a long cold spell.

Joe dashed to the hall telephone and dialled the

9

number of the Morton farmhouse. In a moment he was speaking to Chet Morton, a beefy team-mate on the Bayport High football eleven.

"What's up?" the stout youth asked.

"Get your long johns on," Joe told him. "We're going to whip out to Cabin Island on the *Seagull*. That wind on the bay'll really start your blood circulating!"

Frank and Joe had designed and built the ice-yacht during the previous summer. They had saved their money to buy materials and had worked slowly and carefully on the project. The craft was made so that it could be taken apart and compactly stored in the boathouse where the brothers' motorboat, the *Sleuth*, also was housed.

"Sounds great, but I don't know." Chet hesitated wistfully. "Mom's just mixing a batch of maple fudge."

"Save it till we get back—think of the appetite you'll work up!" Joe added with a chuckle, "Think of your waistline, too. We'll meet you at the boathouse in twenty minutes."

"Well—okay—as long as you don't go poking into any more mysteries."

"No promises, pal!" Grinning, Joe slammed down the receiver before Chet could object.

Moon-faced Chet Morton, who was much fonder of eating and relaxing than he was of dangerous adventures, was constantly bemoaning the Hardys' habit of becoming involved in crime cases. But the stocky youth was a loyal pal and could always be depended on in a tight spot.

After calling Biff Hooper, who agreed to the trip enthusiastically, Joe dressed warmly and hurried outside. Frank was already backing their convertible out of the garage.

The Hardys drove to the boathouse on Barmet Bay. Chet and Biff were waiting for them. Biff, a muscular youth whose hobby was amateur boxing, was dancing about, attempting to persuade plump Chet to spar with him.

Chet held up his hands to fend off the blows. He grinned as Frank and Joe walked towards them. "Glad you're here!" he exclaimed. "This guy is trying to use me for a punching bag!"

"Do you good," Biff rejoined. "Get you in shape!"

Frank laughed. "If you keep this up, Cabin Island won't be big enough for both of you—and us." He gave them hearty slaps on the back. "Let's get going!"

Joe opened the doors of the boathouse and led the way inside. The *Seagull* was chocked on boards which lay over the ice between the cat-walks. Suspended above it in a steel cradle was the *Sleuth*.

From a gear shelf the boys took iron-pointed studs and attached them to their boots, then donned crash helmets and goggles. As they took the ice-yacht outside, the wind whipped hard at their backs. Joe tilted the brake on the outside of the hull, so that the point dug firmly into the ice.

Ten minutes later the four had fastened the long runner plank crossways under the bow, raised the mast, and set sail. Quickly they climbed into the stern's cockpit.

"Strap yourselves in tight," Frank warned as he took the tiller. "That wind's strong and the *Gull's* rarin' to go!"

He released the brake and the sleek white craft glided swiftly out into the bay, now solidly frozen except for the channel, which was kept open by the shipping lines and the Coast Guard.

Cold clear air stung the boys' faces and they were showered with ice chips from the bow runner. They waved to friends who were skating near the shore.

"Where is Cabin Island, anyway?" Biff called to the Hardys.

"In a cove off the bay," Frank shouted, as he guided the *Seagull* in a swooping half circle around a hole that had been cut in the ice by a fisherman.

"Ever been there before?" Chet asked, straining to get his words out against the cold air that whipped across his face.

Joe shook his head. "We've never tried to take our motorboat into that cove. It's shallow and you'd rip the hull unless you knew for sure where every rock is. But we shouldn't have any trouble now."

Presently the ice-yacht raced up the inlet. "We'll go around for a look-see," said Frank.

Skilfully he circled the heavily wooded island. The shoreline facing the bay dropped off in an icy cliff, but the side opposite the mainland road to Bayport sloped gradually. At the edge of the shore Frank spotted a tall pine.

"Let's land there," he said.

He put the speeding craft into a wide semicircle opposite the tree. The sails slackened, the ice-yacht slowed down, then drifted straight to the pine, where Frank put on the brake and Joe lashed the craft to the tree.

"Right on the nose," Biff said admiringly as they clambered ashore.

The four started up the hill. Soon they glimpsed the cabin, perched in a clearing on the highest point of the island.

Joe stopped abruptly and pointed to a set of large bootprints in the light snow. "How can anyone else be here?" he asked. "There's no other ice-yacht here, and it'd be a long, slippery walk from the mainland."

Frank shrugged. "I doubt that the person is still here. It hasn't snowed for a week, so those prints could have been made several days ago."

"But they only lead upward," Joe observed. "There are none going back down the hill."

"Maybe whoever he was went down another way," Frank suggested.

The boys resumed their ascent. As they approached the cabin, a broad-shouldered figure in a plaid mackinaw coat appeared from behind a clump of brush and strode towards them.

He was a surly-looking man in his early thirties, who walked with his neck thrust forward. His off-balance, lumbering gait amused Joe, but the man's words were not funny.

"Get off this island!" he shouted. The Hardys were taken by surprise, but only for seconds.

"Who says?" Joe retorted.

"I say so, and I'll show you!" came the reply as the man thrust his right hand into the mackinaw's deep pocket. He strode closer, glaring at the foursome.

"Don't threaten us!" Biff said angrily, cocking his right fist.

"If it's a fight you want," Frank said coolly, "the odds are one to four. So don't be foolish. Besides, we have permission to be on this island."

The hostile man hesitated, looking from face to face. "What makes you think I don't have permission, too?" he asked. Then the stranger made the mistake of advancing a step farther. Biff feinted with a quick left hand and sent his right fist into the man's midriff. With an "oof" the man sat heavily in the snow, then scrambled to his feet, muttering threats.

"Aw, knock it off," said Chet.

"We won't get anywhere arguing with him," Frank said quietly. "Come on!" The boys turned and retraced their steps to the *Seagull*. Frank and Joe kept glancing back, but the hostile stranger did not follow.

Back in the ice-yacht, Joe said, "I wonder if Mr Jefferson knows that man and gave him permission to come to Cabin Island."

"I doubt it," said Frank. "Say, maybe this has something to do with the mystery."

"Some welcoming committee!" Chet grumbled.

Joe scowled. "He sure was eager to chase us away. I have a hunch he's up to no good."

Soon Frank guided the *Seagull* out of the cove and sent her skimming along Barmet Bay.

Suddenly Chet gasped. "Look at that ice-yacht! Must be a crazy man steering it!"

Heading towards them was a large craft which weaved across the ice in a dizzying path. Suddenly it dipped over and one runner plank lifted off the ice into the air.

"Wow! That's a sharp turn!" exclaimed Frank.

"He'll capsize!" Biff cried out. Just then the pilot dropped the sheet and the runner came down hard, spattering ice.

Joe groaned. "Anybody who gives a boat that slam-bang treatment doesn't deserve to own one."

An instant later the other craft streaked straight for the *Seagull*.

Frank looked grim. "We're in trouble," he said. "That's the *Hawk!*"

The *Hawk* was owned by two belligerent youths, Tad Carson and Ike Nash, who had been in the Hardys' classes at school until they had dropped out early in the term. The two often returned to loiter about the school grounds, bullying younger boys. They were known to be fast, reckless car drivers.

"Ike is steering," Joe observed. "He's even more dangerous on the ice than he is on the road."

"If he doesn't change his course, he'll hit us!" Chet said.

Frank set his jaw. "If Ike won't turn, I will." He bore down on the tiller and swung out of the *Hawk's* path.

A second later the bigger craft also changed course. It was hurtling towards the *Seagull*, gaining momentum every second!

"They mean to run us down!" Biff shouted.

"Or else they just want to scare us," Joe said, clenching his fists.

Frank swerved once more. Again the other steersman mimicked him, and the *Hawk* still came at them. By now it was less than fifty yards away. The boys could see mocking grins on Ike's and Tad's faces. In another few seconds the *Hawk* would crash into the *Seagull*.

Suddenly Ike's grin changed to a look of terror. In a flash Frank realized what had happened. The reckless youth had tried to swerve off the collision course. But the manoeuvre had caused the *Hawk*'s tiller to jam. Ike held up his hands to show that he had lost control of his craft.

In a moment the boats would collide!

·2·

An Angry Caller

FRANK leaned hard on the tiller, while Joe trimmed sail. The *Seagull* veered sharply. The other boys held on so tightly to the gunhales that their knuckles were white. The boat careened, and the ice seemed to leap towards them.

The *Hawk* zoomed past in such a violent rush of wind that Frank thought his craft would surely turn over. But he kept a firm hold on the tiller and Joe eased the sheet. Slowly the craft pulled out of the sharp turn and Frank was able to slow to a stop.

For a moment no one spoke. The boys stared at one another, numb with relief. Then Joe glanced over his shoulder and exclaimed, "They've piled up!"

"Serves them right," Biff declared. "They might have killed us all."

"Still, we'd better go over and see if they're badly injured," Frank said.

The four got out of the *Seagull* and made their way across the ice to the troublemakers, who were surveying the *Hawk*'s broken mast.

Ike Nash limped towards the *Seagull*'s crew, his eyes blazing. "You jerks are going to pay for this damage!" he shouted. "Besides, I'll have to see a doctor about my ankle. It's probably broken. You'll get all the bills, that's for sure!"

"It was your fault," Joe declared. "And if your ankle were broken, Ike, you couldn't walk."

"Save that stuff!" Tad snapped back. "If we wanted to hear a lecture, we'd have stayed in school!"

Biff turned away in disgust. "We can't tell these idiots a thing," he muttered. "Let's go!"

"We may as well," Joe agreed. "Nobody's seriously hurt, so they can make their own way to shore."

The Hardys and their pals headed back for the *Seagull*, ignoring the threats and angry remarks the bullies shouted after them.

"Let's go home," Chet said. "It's almost suppertime, and man, I'm starved!"

The four boarded the craft and sped on towards Bayport. Frank's face wore a thoughtful frown as they glided over the ice.

"What's the matter?" Joe shouted above the wind. "Not worried about those two blowhards back there, are you?"

Frank shook his head. "No, just thinking about that fellow in the mackinaw. I'd sure like to know who he is and what he's doing on Cabin Island."

"Same here." Joe was about to suggest that the quarrelsome stranger might have something to do with the mystery promised by Elroy Jefferson. But, smothering a grin, Joe decided he had better not alarm Chet unnecessarily!

The stout youth almost seemed to read Joe's mind. "I just hope that tough guy isn't around to make trouble if we're going to be spending Christmas vacation on the island," Chet muttered gloomily.

"Don't worry. If he tries anything, we can handle him," Biff said confidently.

Reaching Bayport harbour, they stowed the *Seagull* in the boathouse. Frank locked up and the boys climbed into the Hardys' convertible.

On the way to the farm where Chet lived on the outskirts of Bayport, Joe suggested, "Why not pack our supplies for the trip into the *Seagull* the night before we leave? Then we'll be able to get a quick start."

"But that's Christmas Day!" Biff objected. "We'll want to be home."

"True. How about tomorrow?" Frank asked. "We could pack in the afternoon, in plenty of time for Christmas Eve." This suggestion was agreed upon.

"What shall we bring?" Chet inquired.

"Oh, sleeping bags, extra blankets, snowshoes—that sort of thing," Joe replied.

"And flashlights!" Frank added. "Mr Jefferson did tell me the cabin is primitive—no electricity, no running water. We'll be roughing it."

"I was thinking of the meals," Chet persisted. "Who's in charge of food?"

Frank grinned. "You! But we'll all bring some."

"Sounds fine to me," said Biff, and the others nodded assent.

As they pulled up in front of the Mortons' farmhouse, Chet asked, "What time do we meet tomorrow to pack the *Seagull*?"

"About four o'clock," Joe suggested. "Frank and I ought to be back from our visit with Mr Jefferson by then."

The Hardys next drove Biff to his house. As they headed for their own home, Joe said, "I can't wait to know the details of Mr Jefferson's mystery! Haven't you *any* idea what it's about?"

Frank shook his head. The brothers had become fascinated with detective work at an early age, because their father, Fenton Hardy, was a private investigator whose skill had won him fame all over the country.

Mr Hardy frequently praised Frank and Joe for their ability to recognize significant clues and to make intelligent deductions.

The boys went into the house and found Mr and Mrs Hardy in the living-room. After greeting their parents, Frank said, "I'm afraid Joe and I have a confession. We've made some vacation plans without consulting you."

"I guess we got excited and forgot," Joe admitted. "But it all happened this afternoon."

Tall, muscular Fenton Hardy, his eyes twinkling, winked at his slender, attractive wife. "Laura, do you have the same hunch I do?"

Mrs Hardy smiled ruefully. "Another mystery. Am I right, boys?"

"Yes. But we don't know what kind yet," Frank replied.

The brothers took turns telling of Mr Jefferson's offer. When they had finished, Mr Hardy said, "I think the trip is a reward you deserve."

"Then it's okay, Dad—Mother?" Joe asked.

"All right. But I do hope there won't be any danger."

"We'll be careful," Frank assured her. "Don't worry about us."

"Well," Mrs Hardy said, "I'll have to make a trip to the market for your food supplies."

"You'll have to take a truck to bring home all that food!" exclaimed a tart voice from the doorway. The boys' Aunt Gertrude entered the living-room and added, "I know what it is to feed Chet Morton." She sniffed. "I only hope all you boys won't catch your death of cold!"

Aunt Gertrude was Fenton Hardy's unmarried sister, a tall, angular woman who often made long visits with the family. She liked to affect strictness, and it provoked her that she often found herself smiling when she had intended to be stern with her nephews.

Underneath her peppery manner, Miss Hardy held a deep affection for the boys. She also was interested in their sleuthing, although always predicting dire results.

Joe could not resist teasing her. "Now, Aunty, how about you coming along as our cook?"

"Humph," Miss Hardy mumbled, and hastened to the kitchen.

Soon after supper Frank and Joe excused themselves and went upstairs to pack. "We may as well stow everything aboard the *Seagull* tomorrow except the food," Frank said. "That should give us an early start on Saturday."

The boys stuffed their clothes and gear into duffle bags. Next morning everything was placed in the boot of the convertible.

Shortly after lunch Frank and Joe drove to the Jefferson home, a large colonial dwelling on Shore Road. A housekeeper answered their knock, took their coats, and asked the visitors to be seated in the spacious front hall.

"Mr Jefferson is busy," the woman said. "He will be with you shortly."

After the housekeeper had left, Joe exclaimed in a low voice, "Mother and Aunt Gertrude would sure go for this place! Look at that fancy carved table and gilded work. And those paintings on the walls! The whole house must be furnished in antiques."

"I think it is," Frank told him. "I've heard that Mr Jefferson has a large collection. In fact, he's regarded as an expert on antiques."

Suddenly the boys stopped talking. Loud voices came from the living-room adjoining the hall. The Hardys exchanged quizzical glances.

"Wonder what's going on?" Joe muttered.

"Trouble, from the sound of it," Frank replied.

The speakers seemed to be growing angrier with every sentence. Soon their words were clearly audible.

"I don't understand, Mr Jefferson, why you won't sell. You'll regret this!"

"Cabin Island is not for sale, and that is final, Mr Hanleigh. Now, please leave my home!"

The first voice snapped back, "You haven't heard the last from me!"

Startled, the Hardys stood up. At the same instant a large man stomped into the hall. Frank and Joe were nearly elbowed aside by the angry caller as he strode towards his coat, which was lying on a chair.

The boys nudged each other in excitement. It was the belligerent young man who had chased them off Cabin Island!

As he shrugged violently into his coat, his eyes fell on Frank and Joe. "You two again!" he shouted, glaring at the boys. "Keep out of my way!"

Then he flung open the door and was gone.

·3·

Missing Grandson

"Good afternoon, boys." An elderly man, tall and thin, with shining white hair, stepped into the hall. "I'm sorry to keep you waiting, and also to subject you to Mr Hanleigh's bad manners."

"Oh, we don't mind," Frank said, shaking hands, and added, "I'd like to introduce my brother Joe."

"How do you do, Joe? Boys, I overheard what Mr Hanleigh said to you a moment ago. Whatever did he mean?"

"After you offered us your cabin," Frank explained, "Joe and I were eager to look at Cabin Island, so we went over. Mr Hanleigh was there and ordered us to leave."

Mr Jefferson's smile disappeared and deeper wrinkles formed in his face. He said somberly, "Come in and sit down in the living-room. We'll talk more about this."

Frank and Joe followed their host into a large room, richly furnished with antiques. Heavy, wine-red curtains muted the afternoon sunlight, and a miniature crystal chandelier sparkled at either side of a marble fireplace.

Mr Jefferson motioned the Hardys to be seated in velours-upholstered chairs and went on, "If that fellow Hanleigh shows up while you are staying on the island, you're to chase him off at once!"

"Then you didn't know Mr Hanleigh was on your island?" Frank asked.

"No, indeed," Mr Jefferson replied vehemently. "Mr Hanleigh lives some distance from Bayport. He has come here repeatedly, insisting that I sell Cabin Island to him, but I have refused. Unfortunately, the man is persistent."

"I imagine the island is fairly valuable," Frank commented.

"It is," the elderly man admitted. "But it is not worth as much as the price Hanleigh offers. Besides, the place means more to me than money. My wife and I spent many happy vacations in that cabin with our orphaned grandson, Johnny—my son's boy. And now—" He sighed. "Mrs Jefferson has passed away."

"We're very sorry," said Joe, then added, "It's really great of you to invite us to vacation on Cabin Island."

"Not at all," the old man assured him. "I can't thank you sufficiently for saving my automobile from those thieves. You boys have a great deal of courage."

The Hardys looked embarrassed, and Frank replied, "We enjoyed the case. Joe and I seem to thrive on excitement."

Mr Jefferson's smile changed to an expression of disapproval. "I'm surprised your parents permit you to pursue criminals, however much you appear to—er—thrive on danger," he declared. "I'd never allow my grandson to do such a thing, although he, too, is fascinated by mysterious crimes."

The elderly man's sudden criticism made the Hardys a little uncomfortable. Frank changed the subject and said quickly, "I'd like to hear more about Cabin Island, Mr Jefferson. We weren't there long enough to see much."

Their host relaxed as he spoke of his property. "The cabin itself is well built and cozy, as long as there are logs on the fire. You'll find a good supply of wood in the shed at the back of the cabin. Use all you need."

"I suppose we cook with wood?" Joe inquired.

"Oh, yes!" Mr Jefferson declared with gusto. "The kitchen is warm as toast when the old cooking-stove is stoked up! My wife and I talked of modernizing, but we liked things the way they were, and decided not to. Incidentally, you'll find all the cooking utensils you'll need."

"That's good," Frank said. He hesitated before adding, "Mr Jefferson, may we invite two of our friends to join us?"

"All the better," the old man said with enthusiasm. "The place is large enough. It has two bedrooms, each with a pair of bunks. By the way, how did you fellows get to the island?"

"We have an ice-yacht," Joe explained.

Mr Jefferson frowned. 'Ice-yachts are too risky for youngsters. My Johnny always wanted one, but of course I refused him. Prudence is what young people lack. If my Johnny had learned prudence, things wouldn't be as they are now."

Frank and Joe exchanged quick glances, sensing that the mystery was about to be revealed.

The old man sighed and passed his hands over his

eyes. In a low voice he added, "My Johnny has disappeared!"

The Hardys were both shocked and sympathetic. "That's terrible!" Joe exclaimed, then asked, "How old is Johnny?"

"Fifteen, but he's a big boy. He looks a bit older."

"How long has your grandson been missing?" Frank questioned.

"When I returned from Europe recently," Mr Jefferson replied, "my housekeeper reported that Johnny had left school two weeks before."

"Was he living away from home?" Joe inquired.

"Yes. I've always sent him to boarding school, thinking he'd be safe and in good company. At first I expected that Johnny would return to school, but the headmaster has not heard a word from him."

"Have you, Mr Jefferson?" Frank asked.

"Yes, recently I received a letter from Johnny, saying that he was on a secret mission. The letter was postmarked Dallas, Texas, but the detectives I retain found no clues to him there."

"Have you any idea what he meant by a secret mission?" Frank queried.

"Not the slightest."

"Have you reported Johnny's disappearance to the police?" Joe asked.

"Only the harbour police. My detectives advised me to give the matter as little publicity as possible. And of course I am positive there has been no criminal act. That's why I felt this mystery would be feasible for you boys to work on. There are no dangerous individuals involved."

"Mr Jefferson, you surely don't want us to delay the search for Johnny," Frank said. "We'll postpone our vacation on Cabin Island."

"No, I suggest that you go to Cabin Island because I have a strong feeling it may take a boy to find a boy. Johnny loved the place, and knows every nook and cranny of it well."

Joe nodded. "Sounds like a good spot to start."

Frank asked, "The detectives you mentioned—do they work for you all the time?"

"Yes, I have engaged these two private investigators for quite a while, but for a different reason. They are searching for a priceless collection of antique medals which were stolen from my wall safe two years ago."

"Athletic medals?" Joe asked.

"Oh, no. These were commemorative medals from many lands, made by the world's finest craftsmen. They had been presented by kings and potentates to those who had served with greatness in war and peace."

"An odd hobby," Frank commented.

"And expensive. That's why I'm still continuing the search privately. The police have all but given up."

Upon further questioning by Frank and Joe, Mr Jefferson revealed that his collection comprised twelve medals, kept in a handsome rosewood box. "And when you open it, what a dazzling sight!" the man went on. "Some are set with gems, which sparkle in the burnished metal. And apart from their great beauty, what stories behind each of those medals!" He sighed deeply.

Joe asked, "Could they have been fenced somewhere

—or perhaps sold to a disreputable coin dealer?"

"I think not," came the reply. "My collection was so famous, any dealer would recognize the pieces." He added that all the important dealers knew about the theft.

The Hardys were more fascinated than ever. "Did anything else unusual happen at the time your medals were taken, Mr Jefferson?" Frank asked.

"Amazing. How did you guess? As a matter of fact, something odd did occur then. One of my servants, the houseman—John Paul Sparewell—dropped out of sight and nothing has been heard of him since."

"Quite a coincidence," Joe said. "You think Sparewell may be the thief?"

"I don't like to suspect anyone without proof," Mr Jefferson replied. "But at this point, the detectives and I feel that he probably is. Indeed, it's a most baffling crime. However, you boys aren't to concern yourselves with it."

"But there may be some connection between the missing medals and your grandson's disappearance," Frank suggested.

"The only connection is Johnny's silly notions," Mr Jefferson asserted. "I suppose it was because he heard the detectives discussing the theft of the medals so often at the house here. The boy began to think *he* could solve the mystery, and started seeing clues everywhere. Ridiculous."

"Then Johnny may be working on the case right now!" Joe exclaimed. "Perhaps that's his secret mission."

"You could be right." Mr Jefferson looked very

despondent. "And who knows what harm may come to him! Johnny can be stubborn. When he sets his mind on something, he doesn't give up easily."

The old man sighed wearily and the Hardys felt that further questions might be unwise.

"We must get back now," Frank announced. "Thanks again for your invitation, Mr Jefferson."

Their host smiled wanly, crossed the room, and opened the drawer of a small, ornate table. From it he took a key which he handed to Frank. "Have a fine vacation, all of you!"

"We'll do our best to find Johnny," Joe added, "and let you know of our progress."

They all shook hands, then the boys retrieved their coats and said goodbye.

As the brothers drove away from the Jefferson home, Joe turned to Frank, his eyes gleaming with excitement. "A big assignment!" he declared.

"Just the kind we like!" Frank grinned. "One thing I have a hunch about—Johnny is not in Texas! At least, not now. If he doesn't want to be found, he'd never let on where he really is."

"You're probably right," Joe conceded. "Wow! I wish it were the day after Christmas!"

Frank drove silently for a few minutes, seemingly intent on threading his way through the pre-holiday traffic. But Joe guessed from his brother's expression that the mystery was in Frank's thoughts.

"Give you a penny for 'em," Joe said with a grin.

Frank smiled. "I've been thinking about Mr Jefferson's idea that there are no dangerous individuals involved in this case. I don't agree."

"Why not?" Joe looked puzzled and frowned.

"Joe, two years ago a man disappeared, probably because of those medals. Now a boy who was interested in them is gone. Then Hanleigh turns up, trying to force Mr Jefferson to sell the island."

"I see what you mean. Sounds like the old case is still plenty hot."

Frank nodded. "And with a priceless treasure at stake, we'd better watch out for danger."

·4·

A Christmas Visitor

As the Hardys drove on towards the bay area, they continued to discuss the missing boy.

"Mr Jefferson appears to be very strict with his grandson," Joe observed. "I'm not surprised that Johnny wanted to go off and prove he's old enough to be on his own."

Frank frowned. "Could be. But he's also old enough to realize fully the grief he's causing his grandfather."

Upon reaching their boathouse, Frank parked behind a green car which the Hardys recognized as belonging to the Hoopers. Biff and Chet hopped out to greet their pals.

Joe and Biff unlocked both car boots, and they all looked over the gear each had brought. "It'll take some engineering to stow all this on the *Seagull*," Joe said with a groan.

"And don't forget, we have to leave some space for food," Chet reminded him.

Biff scratched his head. "It's all necessary, including my snowshoes. Chet has his, too."

"You're lucky," Frank replied. "Ours gave out last winter and we haven't had the money to get new ones."

The four boys hauled their gear into the boathouse. The streamlined hull of the *Seagull* had been designed with plenty of space for cargo. Nevertheless, they repacked it three times before they found places for everything. When they had finished, there remained only a few niches for boxes of food.

"That took at least an hour!" Biff exclaimed. "We'd better get going."

Joe locked the boathouse. The friends wished one another a Merry Christmas, and Frank called out, "See you on Saturday!"

At dinner Frank and Joe told their family about Mr Jefferson's mysteries. Mr and Mrs Hardy and Aunt Gertrude expressed concern about Johnny and hoped the missing boy would be found soon.

Frank and Joe went upstairs early in the evening to wrap their gifts before going to bed. In the morning the brothers awakened soon after the sun was up.

"Merry Christmas!" Joe called.

"Same to you!" Frank shouted as he leaped out of bed. The boys dressed and ran downstairs.

"I can smell the turkey roasting already!" Joe exclaimed as he reached the bottom step.

Aunt Gertrude bustled out of the kitchen and scolded cheerfully, "I should hope you do! That gobbler weighs thirty pounds! Now, I've made pancakes and sausage, and I want you both to eat properly before the confusion begins. Oh, Merry Christmas!"

The boys ate the tasty breakfast with zest.

Mrs Hardy looked at her sons. "Mr Jefferson was so kind to make your outing possible," she mused, "it's sad to think of him being alone on Christmas. Why don't we invite him to join us at dinner?"

Joe grinned and said, "Mother, that's a great idea!"

"I'll phone him!" Frank hurried off to make the call.

He returned shortly to announce that Mr Jefferson had accepted the invitation. "I said Joe and I would pick him up on our way back from church."

"Now for our presents!" Joe urged impatiently.

The Hardys went into the living-room where the lights and ornaments shone brilliantly on the tall Christmas tree. The boys were thrilled to discover that their mother had bought each of them a pair of snowshoes. Mr Hardy gave his sons a self-developing camera.

The brothers were overjoyed. "It's terrific! But what's this?" Joe asked, holding up an object that resembled a gunstock.

His father explained that the attachment was a gun-type mounting to use in conjunction with the camera's high-powered telescopic lens. "You should find it very useful for long-range shots," he added. "A number of private investigators have purchased them."

"Thanks!" they chorused, and Frank added, "We'll take it to Cabin Island."

From her sons Mrs Hardy received a colourful skirt and blouse set, Mr Hardy was the happy recipient of handmade doeskin slippers, and Aunt Gertrude beamed over a tan cardigan presented by her nephews.

As for Frank and Joe, they were amused to discover that each had given the other a handsome leather watchband. "I thought you'd like it, because it appealed to me," Joe explained with a wide grin.

"Same here," Frank replied.

"Time for you to open my presents," said Aunt Gertrude as she handed each nephew a brightly wrapped package. "Now you won't catch your death of cold on this foolish winter vacation!"

Joe opened his box first and drew out a pair of full-length red ski underwear! "Well—uh—thanks!" he managed to blurt out.

Frank's gift was the same. "Aunty, I can't wait to wear this!" he said, grinning. He unbuttoned the bright crimson suit and pulled it on over his clothes. Joe did the same, and the boys clowned until even Aunt Gertrude was laughing hard.

When Frank and Joe drove up to the Jefferson home later, the elderly man greeted them with "Merry Christmas, boys!" But there was an agitated ring in his voice.

"Has anything happened, Mr Jefferson?" Frank asked quickly.

The reply was startling. "This morning I found a package on the doorstep. It's a present from Johnny." The old man held up the gift card bearing his grandson's name. "This is Johnny's printing."

The Hardys were astounded. "Is there any clue to where it came from?" Joe asked.

"There's no postmark, so the package wasn't mailed," Mr Jefferson answered, "and none of my neighbours lives close enough to have seen the person who left it, but there is a clue in the gift itself."

From the hall table he took a round box and opened it.

"A can of plum pudding!" exclaimed Joe.

"My favourite dessert," said Mr Jefferson. "But this is the significant thing," he added, pointing to a cluster of fir cones tied clumsily onto the can with red ribbon. "These are blue spruce cones and Cabin Island has many trees of that variety. More than ever, I feel sure my boy is—or was—there."

"Perhaps your housekeeper could tell us when and how the parcel was delivered," Frank suggested.

"No," Mr Jefferson replied. "Mrs Morley is away on a week's vacation."

Mr Jefferson donned his coat and locked the house. Then the three got into the car and Frank started for home. On the way he tried to reassure the distraught man. "Perhaps the gift is a sign that Johnny plans to come home soon. He probably wanted to get back into your good graces before returning."

Mr Jefferson frowned. "That boy won't be back as long as he has the detective bug."

Mr and Mrs Hardy and Aunt Gertrude welcomed their guest warmly, and he soon appeared to relax and enjoy the holiday atmosphere.

By the time Frank and Joe drove their visitor home that evening, he was smiling. As Frank brought the convertible to a stop in front of the Jefferson house, Joe said, "Sir, I have a strong feeling that Johnny is in this area. Will you describe him in detail?"

"I'll do better than that. Come into the house and I'll give you a recent snapshot."

The Hardy boys followed Mr Jefferson up the path. He unlocked the door, stepped into the hall, turned on the light, then cried out in alarm.

Frank and Joe gasped. Furniture had been overturned and drawers hung open, their contents scrambled and strewn about the floor. The antique wall ornaments had been ruthlessly torn down.

The three hurried into the living-room. It, too, was completely disordered. The thick rug was littered with articles that had been in drawers or displayed on shelves. The rich red draperies hung at crazy angles, and one of the crystal chandeliers had been shattered.

Mr Jefferson's face was white and his hands trembled. Frank suggested anxiously, "You'd better sit down, sir. Joe and I will see if the person who did this is still on the premises."

"No, I'll be all right. I have some valuable antiques I must check on immediately. You boys look about."

The Hardys soon discovered that entry had been made by jemmying the rear door. They made a thorough tour of the house and circled the grounds. Although the moon shone brilliantly, the young sleuths could find no clue to the marauder.

"There isn't even a footprint." Joe sighed as he and Frank entered the house again. "Whoever it was evidently went right around the path to the back!"

Mr Jefferson reported that nothing was missing, although many valuable objects had been broken. He handed Frank a snapshot of a tall, well-built boy. "Here is the picture of Johnny."

Frank placed the photograph in his wallet. "You had better report this damage to the police, Mr Jefferson," he advised.

When the elderly man left the room to telephone, Joe murmured, "I know it sounds crazy, but—do you think that possibly Johnny is mixed up in this?"

"No," Frank replied promptly, "I can't believe he's that kind."

A short time later Lieutenant Daley of the Bayport Police Department arrived. He inspected the damage, took fingerprints, and then questioned the Hardys and Mr Jefferson. The officer left, saying headquarters would notify them if any clues to the vandal turned up.

The brothers went to bed as soon as they had told their father about the incident. "We'd better get to sleep pronto if we're going to start early tomorrow," Joe said.

The boys' alarm clock rang just as the sun was rising. Frank and Joe dressed, ate a quick breakfast and gathered their supplies, among which were the Christmas gifts they had received.

Chet and Biff were waiting outside the Hardys' boathouse when the brothers drove up. "Hey!" Joe exclaimed as he and Frank hopped out to meet them. "What's all that?" He pointed to a pile of packages on the ground.

"Our Christmas presents!" Biff replied.

"I got super binoculars," Chet crowed. "And look! A portable ultraviolet light for identifying rocks and minerals."

"How about this?" Biff broke in, holding up a large box. "Barbells! I have the weights, too. And—"

"Fellows!" Frank interrupted. "We'll never fit all this stuff onto the *Seagull!*"

"I see you and Joe brought some of your Christmas loot," Chet grumbled.

"Only what's really needed," Frank insisted. "Snowshoes and a camera. Chet, your binoculars will be great! The rest will have to stay in Bayport."

Biff and Chet gave in grudgingly. "My father drove us here," said Biff. "But you'll have to drive us back to drop these things off."

"Sure. First let's put the food in the *Seagull*," Frank said. The boys did so, then Joe locked the boathouse. The four went off in the convertible and the extra items were returned to the Morton and Hooper homes.

As Frank once more reached the harbour parking area, a startled expression crossed his face. "Didn't you lock up before we left?" he asked Joe.

"Sure I did!" Joe gulped. All four boys stared in disbelief at the area between the parked cars and the Hardys' boathouse.

Their supplies which had been in the *Seagull* were scattered in all directions over the ground!

·5·

Two Suspects

STUNNED, the boys could only stare at one another. Frank turned to Joe and declared, "This reminds me of the damage at Mr Jefferson's place last night!"

"It's too similar to be just coincidence," Joe agreed. "And yet, I can't think of any logical connection between the two break-ins. Who's our suspect, in either case?"

"What are you two talking about?" Chet asked impatiently.

Joe quickly told of the incident at Mr Jefferson's house.

"Goodness! That sounds a lot worse than this mess," said Chet. "Who'd do such a thing?"

"Search me." Joe frowned thoughtfully. "Maybe someone who wants revenge on Mr Jefferson ransacked his house—then found out Frank and I are going to work on his mystery, so the same creep did this to spite us."

"But who?" Chet persisted uneasily.

"What about the wise guy we met on Cabin Island?" Biff put in. "The one who tried to get tough."

Joe shrugged and threw a glance at his brother. "Any hunches, Frank?"

Frank nodded. "I've been wondering about that big fellow myself. We found out his name, by the way—its Hanleigh. He's been trying to buy the island from Mr Jefferson."

Suddenly Joe gave a start. "Say! We ought to check the boathouse! Maybe—" He stopped in mid-sentence and sprinted off. The others followed, catching up to Joe as he unlocked the door and stepped inside.

A chorus of groans came from the boys as they looked from the broken window to the ice-yacht. The sail lay unfurled on the floor and had been slashed. It was completely useless!

"I'd like to get my hands on the skunk who did this!" Biff stormed angrily.

Joe was furious. "Some nerve—smashing his way in!"

Just then a voice spoke from the doorway. "Hi, fellows! What's going on?"

The four turned to see their friend Tony Prito. Tony, a slender, dark-haired youth of Italian descent, stared at the damage with astonishment in his black eyes.

"Hi, Tony," Joe said dejectedly. "We were gone for a short time and just got back to find this mess!"

Tony shook his head. "Tough break! I heard about your trip and came down to see you off."

"Any chance you could join us?" Frank asked. "We'd be glad to sail back for you."

"No, but thanks," Tony replied. "I promised Dad I'd help him out during Christmas vacation and drive one of the trucks." Mr Prito was a busy building contractor in Bayport.

Despite the unpleasant situation, Chet could not

resist a joke. "What's going on in construction this time of year? You building an igloo?"

The others chuckled, and Tony said, "When I pulled up in Dad's truck, I noticed Ike Nash and Tad Carson running down the road from here."

"Ike and Tad again!" Joe exclaimed.

The Hardys' minds filled with questions. Were Ike and Tad the malicious visitors? Did they seek revenge for the damage to the *Hawk* by disabling the Hardys' ice-yacht? Or was there a more sinister motive?

"They're not going to stop us," Joe said determinedly. "Come on! We'll just have to stow all our gear onto the *Gull* again."

"And we need to make repairs," Frank added. "Chet and Biff, will you take our car and pick up the spare sail in our garage? In the meantime, Joe and I will repack."

"Right," Chet agreed, taking the ignition key which Frank handed him.

"On the way," Joe put in, "why not buy us four police whistles? We may need them for signalling on the island."

"And we'd better replace that windowpane," Frank said.

"Don't worry about the glass," Tony said. "I have some spare in the truck. I'll fix the window."

Frank and Joe resumed packing the *Seagull*, while Tony worked on the boathouse window.

As Frank arranged the supplies, he noticed that the seat belts had been cut.

"That's tough," said Joe. "We have no spares."

The boys worked in silence for a while. Then Frank

said, "Joe, this case troubles me. I can't help wondering if there may be something more behind Johnny Jefferson's disappearance than his grandfather suspects."

Joe glanced at his brother keenly. "What do you mean? Do you have a theory?"

"No, not yet. But if Johnny is on Cabin Island—or has been there—his disappearance may be tied in somehow with Hanleigh's desire to buy the place."

"Could be," Joe conceded. "Personally, I'd like to get a line on Ike and Tad. I have a feeling those guys are up to something besides getting even with us—but don't ask me what."

When the Hardys had finished stowing everything aboard the *Seagull*, Tony was picking out the last bits of jagged glass from the window frame. Joe helped him install the new pane, and the Hardys reimbursed their friend for the glass.

"I'd better go now," Tony said. "I'm due to meet Dad on a job. Have a swell time!"

"You bet. Thanks for pitching in," said Frank. Presently he turned to Joe. "I have a hunch that we'll find a lot of answers to the mystery at Cabin Island."

"Yes, if we ever get there!" Joe grumbled impatiently. "One more delay and this'll be a spring vacation!"

Frank grinned. "I think we're in business. Here come Chet and Biff with the spare sail!"

The boys took the *Seagull* outside, where they began replacing the torn sail. They worked dexterously, though their hands grew red and numb from the cold.

"This is a rough job," Biff said grimly.

"It wouldn't be so bad," Frank replied, "but some

of the rigging's been slashed, too." Joe brought a coil of rope from the boathouse and helped his brother repair the damage. Then they reinforced the ruined seat belts with rope.

"Not only did those troublemakers delay us, they've made me wait overtime for my lunch!" Chet complained. "Hey! Was any of the food stolen?"

Frank laughed. "As far as we can tell, Chet, every morsel is intact! Evidently Ike and Tad aren't thieves or gluttons."

"That's the best you can say for them," Biff said scornfully.

"Well, we're set for some hard-water sailing!" Joe announced.

The Hardys replaced their tools in a kit. They made sure that the convertible and the boathouse doors were locked. Then the four put on goggles and helmets. Frank took his place at the tiller while Chet and Biff climbed aboard. Joe shoved the *Seagull* before him with short, running steps until the sail caught the wind.

"Wow! Some load!" he gasped, jumping in beside Frank.

"Full speed ahead for Cabin Island!" Chet cried out. "I'm starving!"

The *Seagull* swooped downwind near the shore of Barmet Bay. It was a clear, sharp day, and the sparkling sun made the ice gleam like glass.

As the boat passed through the narrow inlet and glided towards Cabin Island, Chet chortled. "I'd like to see Hanleigh try to throw us out this time! We have the key!"

"Anyone who causes trouble—let me at him!" Biff sang out gaily.

But Frank looked grave. He pointed to the pine tree where they had parked the *Seagull* on their first visit.

An ice-yacht was outlined against the dark evergreens. "The *Hawk!*"

"It's been repaired," Frank observed.

"And ready for more trouble!" Joe groaned.

Troublesome Trio

FRANK eased the tiller over and made a deft 90-degree turn to port. As the *Seagull* passed the *Hawk*, the boys noted that there was no one in the vicinity.

"Maybe Ike and Tad are hiding," Chet suggested.

"Could be," said Frank. "I'll circle the island and find a more secluded place to tie up."

Joe nodded. "Then we can try to find out what's going on without being seen."

Chet and Biff were disgruntled. "What are that grubby pair doing on Cabin Island, anyway?" Biff asked.

Frank frowned thoughtfully. "Maybe Ike and Tad have some connection with Hanleigh."

Joe nodded. "Perhaps they taxi him to the island whenever he wants to come."

"That's right," Biff agreed. "Last time we were here we wondered how Hanleigh made it without a boat."

"Yes, and he might've been behind their trick on us at the boathouse," Joe said. "I can't figure out, though, how they knew we were heading for Cabin Island today."

Biff grinned. "One more puzzle for us to work on. I

have a feeling that the mystery is getting hotter by the minute!"

Presently Frank slowed the *Seagull* towards a spot on the island's shore where a thick growth of pines and evergreen bushes would conceal the ice-yacht. Then he braked and Joe slackened the sail.

The boys got out and trudged up a slope towards the rear of the cabin. Their footsteps crunched crisply in the snow, but the four Bayporters were careful to keep their voices down.

Suddenly Joe stopped and pointed towards a clearing on the right. "Look! Footprints!"

A line of tracks could be seen all the way to the cabin. Whoever had made them had evidently come up through the clearing from some point along the shore below. Trees farther down the slope, however, blocked the boys' view.

"Maybe Ike or Tad," Chet suggested.

"Or Hanleigh himself," Joe said quietly. "Whoever he is, he must have come here on the *Hawk*."

"Probably," Frank agreed. "Let's make sure, though, before we tackle him. We can backtrack on the prints and find out if anyone came with him."

"Good idea," said Joe.

With Frank leading, the companions followed the footprints downwards to a small, windowless boathouse about a hundred yards from the *Seagull*.

Nearing the building, Frank motioned for silence. Voices could be heard from inside.

The four boys crept closer and soon every word sounded clearly. The speakers were Tad Carson and Ike Nash!

"Hanleigh is sure paying us a lot," Ike was saying. "I'd like to find out what for."

"Who cares, as long as we get our money?" Tad responded lazily.

"Look—figure it out. All we're doing is giving him a boat ride now and then."

"So maybe Hanleigh likes our company."

Ike was evidently becoming impatient with his partner's indifference. "If he likes us so much, why does he make us freeze in this boathouse while he's inside the cabin? I'd like to sneak up there and see what cooks."

"You worry too much, pal," Tad drawled. "We bring him here, we get our money. It's simple."

"Well, stop being simple and maybe we'll learn what's so valuable that Hanleigh's after!" Nash exploded. "We can cash in even more on this deal if we play it right!"

Now his buddy sounded annoyed. "To me, play it right means follow Hanleigh's orders. Trip up the Hardys, stay in the boathouse, don't ask questions."

"You'll do what I say," Ike threatened harshly, "—or else!"

"Okay, cool off," was the quick reply. "Have it your way."

The Hardys and their pals were excited. So Tad Carson and Ike Nash were working for Hanleigh. That was why they had slashed the *Seagull*'s sails!

Frank beckoned the others away from the boathouse. When the four were out of earshot of the troublemakers, he urged, "We'll deal with those two later. Let's go up to the cabin and see what Hanleigh's doing!"

"Right!" Biff declared fiercely. "And if that guy gives us trouble, just let me handle him!"

"Easy, Biff," Frank cautioned. "We'll never learn anything if we tangle with him."

Quietly the boys climbed the tree-covered slope. At the edge of the woods they stopped and peered at the cabin. Stealthily the quartet moved to a window and looked into the long living-room at the front of the building.

Hanleigh stood with his back to the boys, facing a huge stone fireplace. He held a measuring tape and was apparently determining the dimensions of various sections of the stone chimney. Frequently he paused to write in a small notebook.

The big man began to pace back and forth, then stood still. By the motions of his right forefinger, the watchers could tell that he was counting the stones in the height and width of the fireplace, mantel, and chimney. Finally he got down on hands and knees and explored the interior of the fireplace.

Once Hanleigh shook his head as if baffled. The boys were so intrigued, they unconsciously crowded closer to the window until their faces were pressed against the pane.

Suddenly a gust of wind blew open the door of the cabin, which Hanleigh evidently had left ajar. Startled, the man leaped to his feet and whirled around. He glanced towards the door, then gave a shout of consternation, glimpsing the boys a second before they ducked out of view.

Hanleigh strode across the room and rushed outside. "Hold your ground!" Frank advised his companions.

"Don't let him bluff us. He shouldn't be here."

The intruder was red with wrath as he confronted the boys. "Can't you pests mind your own business?" he snarled. "I told you to stay off this island!"

"So you did," Frank returned coolly.

"Then what are you doing here?" roared Hanleigh. "You're a bunch of meddlers! Now, get out! And if I catch you again, I'll—"

"You'll do nothing, Mr Hanleigh," Joe interrupted. "You have no right to be on this island, but we have."

"Prove that!" Hanleigh scoffed.

Joe took the key to the cabin from his pocket and said, "Mr Jefferson gave this to us. Do you have a key, too? Or did you break in?"

"Young punks!" the man snarled.

Quickly Joe examined the front door and saw that it had not been forced. "My guess is that Mr Hanleigh has a skeleton key," he said. "The lock is a simple one."

The intruder flushed but said nothing.

"Suppose you tell us what's so interesting about Cabin Island, Mr Hanleigh," Frank suggested. "And what's special about the fireplace?"

Hanleigh licked his lips nervously. "Jefferson collects antiques. Maybe I collect fireplaces, that's all. I made him a good offer for this place. He's a fool to turn it down."

"Well, stay off this property!" Joe snapped. "Mr Jefferson instructed us to order you to leave if we found you here."

Hanleigh clenched his fists and glared at the boys. "Think you're pretty smart! Well, you fellows are going to be sorry! This spooky place is no picnic. You'll be glad to clear out!"

Before the boys could retort, the man turned on his heel and strode down the hill towards the boathouse. The sleuths watched from outside the cabin until they saw the *Hawk* glide out of the cove into the open bay with the trio aboard.

"We made short work of that crew!" Biff said cheerfully.

The Hardys did not comment, but inwardly felt certain they had not seen the last of Hanleigh.

"Short work nothing!" Chet exclaimed. "It's starting to get dark, and we still haven't had lunch! Come on, have a heart! I need supper."

"You won't be able to eat until we get our supplies unloaded and organized," Frank reminded him.

Joe grinned. "I'm starved, too. Let's get the stuff."

Everyone set to work with a will and plodded back and forth between the *Seagull* and the cabin. Joe noticed that Chet was less talkative than usual. "Thinking about your meal?" he asked.

Chet shivered. "Not now. I'm thinking about Hanleigh's warning. What did he mean about 'this spooky place'?"

"Probably meant it's haunted," Biff said sombrely. "You wouldn't mind a couple of ghosts for company, would you, Chet?"

"Cut it out!" Chet quavered, glancing around into the deepening shadows.

"If there's a ghost here, I wish he'd show himself," Frank put in, chuckling. "We could use an extra hand. But this should be the last load." He let the main sheet go completely, so the sail would be free to swing in the wind.

The four were halfway to the cabin, their arms filled with provisions, when suddenly Chet stopped short and gave a startled cry. The provisions he had been carrying fell to the ground.

"What's wrong?" Joe asked.

For a moment Chet could only point. Then he declared in a strange, hollow voice, "There! In the woods! A ghost!"

·7·

Cry for Help

CHET stood rooted to the spot. He kept staring straight ahead. The other boys looked but could see no sign of the ghost.

Finally Joe said, "You sure talked yourself into that one, Chet."

"What do you mean?"

"Mr Hanleigh planted the idea in your mind and your old brain conjured up a ghost for you," Joe explained.

Chet looked scornful. "Is that so? Well, you're wrong, Joe Hardy. I saw a ghost."

Frank winked at his brother to stop his needling. To Chet he said, "Let's get to the cabin—and some food."

The trudge was continued without any further evidence of a ghost. When the boys reached the living-room of the cabin, Joe lighted a large oil lamp that stood on the table, and a mellow glow spread over the room.

Chet declared he felt better, but added, "Honest, fellows! I did see this white thing—moving l-like a ghost!"

Frank spoke up. "Okay. Biff and I will go out and take a good look around while you and Joe put away our things and start supper."

"Fine idea!" Joe agreed. "I was thinking that we ought to appoint Chet cook, anyway. Then we'll never miss a meal!"

Chet brightened at once. "Kitchen, here I come!" he said with enthusiasm.

Frank and Biff rummaged among the gear for flashlights before leaving the cabin.

"This'll be a good chance to go over the island thoroughly," Frank remarked to his brother. "I still have a hunch that Johnny Jefferson may have come here."

"You could be right," Joe agreed. "If we're lucky, maybe you'll pick up a clue."

"Be on your guard," Chet cautioned as Frank and Biff started out the door.

"Don't worry, we'll keep our eyes open—especially for spooks!" Biff called back over his shoulder.

When the two boys had left, Joe went into the kitchen, opened the back door, and discovered the woodshed Mr Jefferson had mentioned. It was an enclosed lean-to and had a door that locked with an outside bolt.

Joe carried enough wood into the cabin to stoke both the living-room fireplace and the cooking-stove. Soon the cabin began to warm up and Joe and Chet removed their heavy parkas.

Chet lighted the oil lamp which stood on the kitchen table and unpacked enough of the food for several meals. "I'll leave the rest in the boxes," he said, and set them on the bottom shelf in the cupboard.

Meanwhile, Frank and Biff had decided to separate in order to scout the whole area more quickly. Each was to search half the island, then meet the other boy at the boathouse.

"Watch out for white things!" Biff warned jokingly.

"You mean like snowballs?" Frank returned with a grin. "Seriously, Chet may not have imagined that spook—so don't take any chances, Biff. If you spot anything suspicious, give a blast on that police whistle."

"Wilco!"

The two boys started off in different directions. Frank trudged through the crusted snow, playing his flashlight beam ahead of him among the pines and underbrush. The wind had picked up, its icy chill stinging his face to a raw numbness.

As Frank plodded on through the dusk, he stopped to listen as each new sound caught his ear. Once he was sure he had heard someone cough and hurried in its direction. Nobody was in sight. But just then, an owl flew past, and Frank jumped back startled.

"I'm getting as jittery as Chet," Frank berated himself. He squared his shoulders and went on, beaming his light.

Half an hour later the two searchers met at the boathouse. "Any luck, Biff?"

"None, Frank. Cabin Island evidently has visitors only in the daytime. How about you?"

"I didn't find a clue, but I—" Frank stopped speaking as an object on the ground caught his attention. He bent over to pick it up.

"Wow!" said Biff. "A model of an ice-yacht."

"And expertly carved," Frank remarked, examining the intricately made model.

"Do you think Tad or Ike or Hanleigh lost this?"

Biff asked. "Or could it belong to Mr Jefferson?"

Frank examined the little boat, then declared, "It probably belongs to some very recent visitor to the island. The wood doesn't look as though it has been exposed to the elements very long. In fact, it seems to be newly carved."

"Anyway, it's a beauty," Biff commented. "Why don't you take it along and put it on the cabin mantel?"

It was fully dark by the time Frank and Biff reached the cabin and reported that they had found no one on the island.

"Well, I'm willing to forget the ghost, now that we're about to eat," Chet called from the kitchen.

"How long before chow's ready?" Frank asked. "The wind has started to blow pretty hard. I'd like to take the *Seagull* around to the boathouse."

"You have time," Chet replied. "But hurry."

Frank showed Joe and Chet the ice-yacht model, then set it on the mantel before stepping outside and hurrying to the shore. Quickly he jumped into the ice-yacht and trimmed the sail. The instant the brake was released, the craft glided off like a phantom and in a short time Frank reached the boathouse. It was unlocked and empty. The boy stored the boat inside, then tramped back to the cabin.

There he found Joe and Biff staring at the massive stone chimney. "We're trying to figure out what interested Hanleigh," Joe remarked.

"Beats me," Biff added.

Chet interrupted from the kitchen. "Chow time!" he called, and ushered his friends to the table on which stood bowls of steaming beef stew. There was plenty of creamy milk and a big basket of warm, crusty bread.

"Delicious!" exclaimed Biff after tasting the stew. "I'll bet that ghost was just hungry and hoping for an invitation!"

"It's an old family recipe," Chet boasted.

"You mean an old family can opener?" Joe rejoined. "I saw all those cans you brought!"

"I had to add special spices, though, and salt and pepper," Chet said defensively. "That's what makes it taste so good."

When the meal was finished, Biff was elected dishwasher. "Scrub hard and you'll develop your boxing biceps," Chet teased. Frank volunteered to help, and soon the kitchen was in order.

The wind was howling louder now, but the interior of the cabin was snug. The boys sat in front of the briskly burning logs in the fireplace and listened to the creaking of low branches against the cabin.

"I wish we could learn what Hanleigh hopes to gain by coming to this place," Joe mused, "or by purchasing it."

"One thing I'm convinced of," said Frank. "He wasn't studying the fireplace just for its artistic look."

"He's certainly nervy with other people's property," Biff remarked.

Frank nodded. "I keep wondering if it was he who ransacked the Jefferson home."

"Again, the question is why?" Joe said.

"I'd think you guys would be more worried about that ghost I saw pussyfooting around here," Chet spoke up plaintively.

"What's more important," said Frank, "is that we

don't forget the mystery we're supposed to solve, to find Johnny Jefferson. Joe and I believe he's hiding in this area."

Joe added, "I've a hunch this mystery will be solved near Bayport. Johnny is bound to run out of money, and if he looks for a job, somebody will become suspicious because he's so young."

"Besides," Frank said, "if we stick to our theory that Johnny is searching for the stolen medals, we can be pretty sure he hasn't given up. Not if he's as keen on sleuthing as his grandfather says he is. As far as we know, no one has located Mr Jefferson's collection or the servant suspected of stealing it."

Biff looked puzzled. "I'm glad we're going to stay. But what's this talk about stolen medals and a suspected servant? You've been holding out on us."

"Yes, explain!" Chet gave the Hardys a sideways look. "I have a feeling that once again you two have taken me along on a double-headed mystery!"

The brothers related the story of the missing rosewood box and the priceless collection of honorary medals. As Joe told of the suspect, and of Johnny Jefferson's desire to be a detective, the storm suddenly grew in violence. Snow hissed against the windows and the sashes rattled ominously.

Then, in the distance, the boys heard a muffled crash.

"A big tree must have gone down!" Joe exclaimed.

Frank looked at the fire. "Let's each bring in an armload of logs before we go to bed. This is going to be a long, cold night."

The four donned their parkas and took flashlights.

Pushing hard, they managed to open the back door and hurried to the woodshed. Abruptly the boys stopped and listened intently. Through the darkness and the wind-driven sleet and snow came a faint cry.

"*Help!*"

·8·

The Mysterious Messenger

STARTLED, the boys stood motionless in the swirling snow, scarcely able to believe that someone was crying for help on the dark, ice-locked island.

Then the faint sound came again above the tearing wind. "Help!"

"Where's it coming from?" Biff asked anxiously.

"Hard to tell," Frank replied. "Let's fan out and make a search. Hurry!"

Each boy started off in a different direction. When the pleading cry was repeated, Joe shouted as loudly as he could, "Fellows! This way! Down by the shore!"

He kept following the call for help, trudging through the blowing snow which stung his face. The flashlight's beam did not penetrate the dense whiteness, and Joe could barely see a step ahead. Frequently he tripped over roots and nearly went sprawling.

Joe was becoming uncertain of his direction. Perhaps his ears had played tricks on him!

The young sleuth stood still until he heard the desperate voice again. "Help!"

"This way!" shouted Joe, moving forward, certain that the cries were coming from somewhere near the boathouse.

Who could the person be? What was he doing on Cabin Island? How could anyone have crossed the ice in the violent storm? Joe beamed his light about in hopes that the other boys would find him.

All at once he realized that the surface had become level and slippery beneath his feet. "I must have stepped onto the ice," Joe thought, and made his way back to land. Where *was* the stricken person? He must be close by!

A groan came suddenly from Joe's left. Moving the flashlight in a slow arc, he called out, "Hello? Where are you?"

There was another moan, which tailed off weakly. As the youth moved towards the sound, his foot struck something soft. Joe dropped to his knees and flashed the light downwards. The beam revealed a stranger, barely conscious, his legs pinned beneath the limb of a fallen pine tree.

The man had gone face downwards and his right check was crunched into the snow. Joe scrutinized him, but could not place the man from what he could see of his features.

"Frank! Biff! Chet!" Joe called out again. "Here, by the boathouse!"

Meanwhile, Joe attempted to free the victim, but all his strength could not budge the heavy branch. To lift it, the whole tree would have to be levered.

"I'll just have to wait for the others," Joe realized, panting. He crouched alongside the man, trying to shield him from the biting wind and the snow.

At last Joe saw the dim glow of flashlights moving down the slope. "Over here!" he called. "Hurry!"

"Joe!" came Frank's voice above the wind. "I can see your beam now! We're coming!"

Biff and Chet were close behind Frank, and the three soon reached Joe and the stranger.

"Who is he?" Chet puffed excitedly.

"I never saw him before," Joe replied. "See if you fellows can hoist this branch a bit so I can pull his leg free."

While Joe continued to shelter the man, the others laboriously managed to raise the tree limb.

"Okay—that'll do it!" Joe said, easing the victim free. "Now let's get him to the cabin pronto."

As gently as possible, the Hardy boys lifted the stranger and started up the slope—Joe supporting the man's head and shoulders, while Frank carried his legs. Chet and Biff went on ahead to light the way and forge a trail through the drifting, deepening snow.

Inside the cabin, Frank and Joe placed the limp form on the sofa. "The poor fellow may be in shock from exposure and pain," Frank declared. "Chet, bring some blankets. No—don't prop him up, Biff! Keep his head low."

"Shall we try to take off his jacket?" Joe asked.

"No," said Frank. "We don't want to move him too much. I'll just loosen the jacket."

Frank did so and also pulled off the man's boots and cap. The stranger's hair was bristly and carrot-coloured. His round face was blanched, but its rough, weather-beaten features, thickly peppered with freckles, gave him the look of an outdoorsman.

The boys covered their patient with blankets and rubbed his hands and feet to stimulate the circulation.

As gently as possible, Frank and Joe lifted the stranger.

"He's mighty pale!" Chet whispered fearfully.

"What do you suppose he's doing out here on a night like this?" Biff asked.

"We'll have to wait until he's able to tell us," Joe replied, and added, "I wish we knew if there are any bones broken."

"We can't get him to Bayport until this storm lets up," Frank said ruefully.

Presently the man began to stir and attempted to mumble something. "Take it easy. You're all right," Joe said soothingly.

The victim began to make weak, convulsive motions, and his mouth twitched. Finally he gasped, "Message—Hardys!"

Frank and Joe exchanged glances of astonishment. Why had the man spoken their name?

The stranger, with a painful effort, articulated, "Must bring—message—to—Hardy boys!" Utterly exhausted, he lapsed into unconsciousness.

"A message!" gulped Chet. "From whom?"

Frank shook his head. "I've never seen this man before."

"We'd better learn about the message," Joe declared. "It must be urgent!"

The Hardys gently explored the victim's pockets, but found nothing. "We'll have to wait until he can tell us," Frank finally conceded.

"Trying to speak may have been too much for him," Joe said with concern. The man's breathing had become irregular, and his pallor had increased.

"His hands feel so cold!" Chet murmured.

"It's probably from shock and exposure," Frank

told him. "We'll just have to keep him quiet and warm until we can get him to a doctor."

The stranger soon began to mumble again, but what he said was unintelligible. The boys kept an anxious vigil for an hour. At last the man gave a sigh and began to breathe more deeply and regularly. A little colour returned to his face.

"I think he's sleeping normally now," Frank said. "He's worn out."

"So am I!" Chet exclaimed with a yawn. "What a day! Let's go to bed."

"We can't leave this man alone," Joe objected. "We'll have to take turns watching him."

"You're right," Frank agreed. "Besides, someone should keep an eye on the fire. We can't let it go out tonight! I'll stand first watch."

Everyone agreed, and Frank sat by the fire while the others prepared their sleeping bags. Chet and Biff shared the north bedroom. The Hardys were to occupy the one across from it.

The patient continued to sleep soundly, and after two hours, Frank placed a large log on the fire and went to rouse his brother. "Your turn!" he told Joe. "All's well!"

Joe put on a bathrobe and took his place near the fire. The snow had stopped, but the wind was still tearing viciously at the trees and cabin.

As time passed, questions again filled Joe's mind. Where was Johnny? What was Hanleigh's interest in Cabin Island? Did the two have any connection? Who was the injured man and what did his cryptic utterance mean? Who had sent the message?

"Lots of questions but no answers," Joe thought with a feeling of frustration. He scowled intently into the fire burning steadily in the grate.

Gradually the warmth radiating from the fireplace, together with the comforting hiss and crackle of the logs, had a soothing effect. The mystery continued to nag at Joe's brain, but he found it harder and harder to focus his thoughts.

"Boy, Chet can sure saw wood!" he said to himself with a grin as a faint sound of snoring drifted from the north bedroom. At last Joe's own eyelids began to droop.

Suddenly the young sleuth gave a start and leaped to his feet. Somewhere in the cabin an eerie noise was shrilling. "Owoooooo!"

Joe did not move, but tensely looked around the room. The weird sound began again with a plaintive quality that was almost human. What could it be?

The boy sternly told himself, "I'm imagining things! It must be one of the fellows. Biff's playing a practical joke on poor old Chet!"

"Owoooooo!" came the wail once more.

Joe walked softly into the bedroom, resolved to surprise the prankster. To his astonishment, he found both Chet and Biff wide awake in their bunks, worried looks on their faces. The two youths were sitting upright and listening to the sound which moaned and then rose to a howl.

"W-what did I t-t-tell you?" Chet quavered. "Th-the ghost—it's right here in the cabin!" He burrowed into his sleeping bag like a rabbit diving for its hole.

The noise came again just as Frank strode in to join

them from the Hardys' bedroom across the hall.

"Sure is unnerving!" Biff admitted, glancing about uneasily.

"We're going to find out what's happening," Frank declared. "If this is somebody's idea of a joke, I want to get my hands on him."

"You said it!" Biff's momentary apprehension vanished. "We'll rout out that phony spook and really give him something to joke about!"

As the lanky youth hopped out of bed, Chet spoke up fearfully, "Be careful, you guys! You may be asking for all kinds of trouble!"

Frank and Biff donned bathrobes. Then with Joe they took up flashlights and searched the cabin for the source of the sound.

In the kitchen Joe cast his light on the ceiling beams. "I think it's coming from somewhere up in the rafters!" he said.

The sinister shriek seemed to grow louder with every gust of wind.

"You're right!" Biff agreed.

The boys moved their flashlights slowly over the ceiling. Suddenly Frank exclaimed, "Yes, look!" He pointed out thin lines forming a rectangle across the boards.

"It must be a trap door!" Joe said excitedly.

"To the attic, I suppose," Frank reasoned.

He grabbed a chair, stood on it, and pushed the trap door open. "I'll need a boost," he said.

Biff gave him a lift. Frank scrambled into the dark opening, then disappeared. His footsteps made the boards creak ominously above Joe and Biff.

The wailing noise came again with a kind of taunting quality. "Owoooooo-oo!"

"Hey, what's going on?" Joe called out.

There was no response.

·9·

Warning by Code

Joe broke out in gooseflesh as the wailing abruptly ceased. The attic floor creaked again and Frank looked down through the opening into the kitchen. "I've captured the ghost!"

"No kidding. Show me," Biff said.

"Here!" Frank replied. He handed down an empty lemonade bottle.

"What do you mean?" Joe asked as Frank swung himself through the open trap door and dropped to the floor.

"Listen," Frank said.

He held the neck of the bottle to his lips and blew hard. The others heard a low, thin version of the doleful sound that had terrified Chet.

"Where did you find this?" Biff asked.

"The bottle was being used to plug a hole in the roof," Frank explained. "When the wind blew across it in a certain way—it hooted!"

Joe laughed. "I wonder if Hanleigh heard that sound and that's why he said the place has spooks!"

Frank took a piece of wood from the box beside the stove. "This'll do to plug the opening," he said. With a boost from Joe, he went into the attic again. After plugging the hole, he lowered himself onto Joe's shoulders and closed the trap door before jumping down.

The three returned to the north bedroom. Biff pulled Chet from his cocoon of blankets. "Here's your wailing ghost," he said, handing the lemonade bottle to his friend. Then he explained how the wind had produced the noise.

Chet placed the bottle on the floor and gave the others a scornful look. "Maybe this is what we heard," he said, "but it's not what I saw running through the woods in a white sheet!"

"Now that you're awake, Chet, why don't you take your turn standing guard?" Joe suggested.

"Oh, all right!" Chet grumbled, crawling from bed. When he reached the living room, he called out, "Hey, everybody! Come here! Our patient is waking up!"

The three rushed to the sofa. "W-where am I?" the stranger asked, blinking his eyes and staring in bewilderment at the boys' faces hovering above him.

Joe took a match and lighted the paraffin lamps, then sat on the floor beside the sofa.

"Easy," he cautioned. "You had a close call!"

"The sudden storm!" the man muttered. "The wind and the snow—I couldn't see—"

"We know," Joe said soothingly. "But you're safe now, and the storm is over." The boys realized for the first time that the wind had stilled.

"How do you feel?" Frank asked.

"I'm all right," the man insisted, as he started to rise.

"Be careful!" Chet warned, but the stranger

chuckled and sat upright. They noticed that the man's eyes were bright blue, and had a merry twinkle.

"You may be injured," Frank said. "Please lie down. We can take you to see a doctor."

"I don't need any doctor!" the red-haired man declared cheerfully. "I feel a little sore and I must have bumped my head, but that'll do no damage!" He moved his arms and legs. "See? I'm okay."

"Who are you?" Frank inquired again.

"My name is Mack Malone. Call me Mack."

The boys introduced themselves and the man's face crinkled into a big grin. "So you're the Hardys!" he said to Frank and Joe. "I came out to give you a message."

"Who sent you?" Joe asked excitedly.

"Your father," Mack replied. "You see, I often do errands for the Bayport police. Fenton Hardy asked me to bring his sons a message. I drove my car to the mainland road across the cove from here and walked over on the ice."

"Didn't you realize the danger?" Joe asked.

"The storm hit suddenly. For a while I nearly gave up. But then I thought I'd finally reached Cabin Island. The ground was so slippery I couldn't get out of the way of that falling tree."

"Lucky we found you," said Joe. "What was the message—?"

Mack Malone chuckled. "It's a funny one—doesn't seem worth the trouble we've all been through! Well, here it is: '*The alley cat is after the mice, but feed him well!*' "

"Very strange!" Joe commented.

"I'll say!" Frank agreed.

"Boy! It's a riddle to me!" Chet declared, then added, "It's almost daylight, and you Hardys will probably puzzle your brains over that message, anyway. How about some breakfast?"

"Good idea!" Biff agreed.

The boys dressed and a short time later Mack Malone joined them for a hearty meal of fried eggs, bacon, and toast. When they had finished, the man stood up and said, "Well, fellows, the sun is rising. I'd better be on my way."

"We'd be happy to take you to Bayport for a checkup," Frank reminded him.

"No, thanks. I'm fit as a fiddle, except for a few bruises," the red-haired man assured him. "I'll stroll over to my car and be home in no time!"

"Watch your step crossing the ice," Joe cautioned.

"You bet your boots I will!" Malone gave a wry laugh and added, "One accident is enough—and besides, I'd sure hate to spend New Year's Day on crutches!"

"Thank you for bringing the message," Frank said as their visitor left the cabin. Malone responded with a parting wave.

When he was out of sight, Biff turned to the Hardys. "What about that double-talk?" he questioned. "Do you really believe your father would send a man to tell you some nonsense about cats and mice?"

"Somebody's pulling your leg!" Chet put in.

"No, it's on the level," Frank assured them. "Joe and I were pretending we didn't understand while Mack was here. Dad sent the message in code because he wanted it to be kept secret for his own reasons."

"Then what does it mean?" Chet asked impatiently.

"That someone is out to get Frank and me—we're the 'mice,' " Joe explained. "We're to play along with the person—he's the 'cat'—and trap him. In other words, 'feed' him and avoid being 'eaten' by him!"

"Fine!" declared Biff. "But who is this cat? How will you find out?"

"We already know," Frank said.

"You do!" Chet exclaimed.

"Dad frequently uses the phrase about the cat in secret communications to us," Joe explained. "The clue is in the adjective. Here, it's 'alley cat'—the second syllable, 'ley,' could stand for the 'leigh' in Hanleigh!"

"Wow!" Chet was wide-eyed. "So Hanleigh *is* out to get you!"

"How does your dad know?" Biff asked.

Joe shrugged. "He must suspect the fellow is after something in the cabin or on the island."

"Hanleigh's a rough customer," Frank said grimly. "That's probably why Dad used code. He was afraid Hanleigh might intercept Mack and force the message from him."

Chet groaned. "Maybe we ought to pack up and go home while we can!"

"We can't leave," Frank insisted. "If Hanleigh is trying to steal something from Mr Jefferson, we must stop him."

"But aren't you supposed to keep looking for Johnny?" Biff asked. "And he doesn't seem to be on Cabin Island. So what do you do next?"

"First, I'd like to search more thoroughly," Frank

replied, "to make sure Johnny hasn't come here since yesterday."

The boys donned their outdoor clothes and spread out over the whole island. Each examined a separate area, searching among bushes, trees, and rocks. Then they combed the entire shoreline. When they finally rejoined each other, none had any clues to report.

After they returned to the cabin, Chet asked, "Now what?"

"We could investigate the mainland near here, and inquire if anyone has seen Johnny," Frank proposed.

"But I'm wary of leaving the place unguarded, especially after getting Dad's message," Joe said with a look of concern.

"We can use my binoculars from the mainland," Chet reminded him, "to keep an eye on the island while we're away."

"Good idea!" Joe exclaimed. "And I'll bring the camera Dad gave us. Maybe we'll get some good photos with the telescopic lens."

Frank remarked, "Our going away might lure Hanleigh here, and that may be what Dad wants."

"Let's have lunch before going off on this wild-goose chase," Chet urged. "I'll make some sandwiches."

"Good and thick, please," Biff begged. "All that tramping around has really given me an appetite!"

"Same here," said Joe.

The boys ate quickly, then set off in the *Seagull*. The strong wind of the previous evening had blown most of the snow to the land, so the ice-yacht tacked across the surface at a fast clip.

Looking back at the island, Chet remarked, "It's sure a pretty place."

Tall pines looked like white pyramids, and bare branches were coated with ice which glittered in rainbow colours.

On the mainland directly opposite, the four boys spotted a shack built of sun-bleached boards. Smoke was drifting upward from its rickety stove-pipe chimney.

Frank slackened sail and let the *Seagull* drift to a complete stop.

"Let's talk to the person who lives here," he suggested, putting down the brake.

A bearded man came out and called, "What can I do for you?"

"We're looking for a boy who is missing from his home in Bayport," Joe replied. "His name is Johnny Jefferson. He's fifteen, and big for his age."

The shack owner shook his head. "I haven't seen a soul as long as I've been here this winter. Say, have you asked Pete Hagen? He lives in a fishing hut just about a mile down shore."

Frank thanked the man and sailed the *Seagull* in that direction. The boys found Hagan fishing through the ice just beyond his home. He had seen no boy of Johnny's description.

As the four companions glided away, Joe said, "This is discouraging. Only thing we can do is cruise up and down the coast."

Frank worked skilfully to keep the vessel close to shore while Biff scanned the woods with his binoculars. "No one's in there," he reported.

"Let's hike up that hill," Joe finally suggested,

pointing to a section where pine trees grew down to the shoreline of the inlet. "From the top we can see Cabin Island and keep an eye on it."

Frank brought the *Seagull* in and braked it. The boys strapped on snowshoes and made their way up the densely wooded slope. At the top, they found themselves in the back yard of a weathered log cabin which perched on the edge of the precipice.

"Wonder who lives here," Biff said.

"No one, from the looks of it," Frank replied. "But let's go see."

The four approached the cabin. It was small and crudely built, with large chinks between the logs. The place had a desolate appearance.

The boys knocked several times at the door, then Joe went to look through a window. "I think the place has been abandoned," he reported. "There's not much furniture, and everything is covered with dust."

"Let's go in!" Chet urged. "My feet hurt and I'm freezing!"

"I suppose if nobody's living here, it's all right," said Frank. He tried the door, which opened creakily.

The boys took off their snowshoes and went inside. At once Chet plopped into a sagging easy chair. A cloud of dust spewed up from the faded cushions. He coughed and the others laughed.

"What a view!" exclaimed Biff, looking out the front window. Below, the curve of Barmet Bay lay like an ice-blue jewel, with Cabin Island a white pearl in the distance. Biff focused the binoculars on the spot. Suddenly, he cried out, "Hey, fellows! An ice-yacht is pulling up to the island! It's the *Hawk!*"

· 10 ·

Puzzling Theft

BIFF's report on the ice-yacht sent a thrill of excitement through the Bayporters.

"Who's aboard?" Frank asked eagerly.

"Hanleigh and his two stooges," Biff replied. "He's climbing out now, but Ike and Tad are staying in the boat."

Biff handed the binoculars to Frank. Clamping them to his eyes, he saw Hanleigh moving alone up the slope towards the cabin. A sudden inspiration struck Frank.

"Let's get the goods on him, Joe. How about using your self-developing camera? You can photograph Hanleigh from here with the telescopic lens."

"Great idea!" Joe exclaimed. "He'd probably deny he was on this island. If we have proof he was there, we may be able to bluff him into telling us what he's after."

Joe, too, took a hasty look through the binoculars before passing them on to Chet, then removed the camera from its case, focused it, and clicked the shutter. "I'll leave the print in the camera until we get back. Let's go!"

"Wait a second!" exclaimed Frank, who had taken over the glasses again.

"What's Hanleigh doing now?" Biff asked as Frank shifted the binoculars slightly.

"He's circling the cabin—hey! He's stopping at the chimney! Looks as if he's examining it."

Hanleigh had a stick with which he tapped and poked at the stonework. Presently he stopped and disappeared among the trees.

"Bet he's leaving," said Frank. "Come on, fellows!"

The boys hurried from the cabin, donned their snowshoes again, and made their way down the slope. Soon they reached the *Seagull*. All climbed aboard except Biff who pushed the ice-yacht to a running start.

As the *Gull* swooped across the cove to Cabin Island, Joe pointed toward the entrance to the bay. "Hanleigh's leaving. There goes the *Hawk!*"

Biff turned the binoculars on the speeding craft and shook his head. "Hanleigh isn't aboard. Ike and Tad are alone."

"Hanleigh must still be on the island!" Joe cried out. "Hurry, Frank!"

"Right!" His brother skilfully manoeuvred the *Seagull*, taking full advantage of every gust of wind. "No doubt Ike and Tad will come back for Hanleigh later," Frank added as he steered for the boathouse.

"Later? It's nearly evening already!" Chet observed. "I'll bet that guy plans to stay all night!"

Biff hooted. "Where would he sleep? Under a rock?"

Joe looked thoughtful. "Maybe you have something, Chet. Hanleigh may know of a secret shelter on the island—perhaps a cave somewhere along the shore."

Frank brought the *Seagull* to the boathouse, and as

he put it inside, the boys discussed the strange action of Ike and Tad.

"I wonder why they took off," Joe said. "We heard them agreeing to spy on Hanleigh, but now for some reason they seem to have changed their minds."

"Maybe those two have deliberately stranded Hanleigh!" Frank exclaimed.

"You mean," said his brother, "Ike and Tad tried to cash in on Hanleigh's deal, and he told them to get lost."

"Right," said Frank. "So now they're getting even by leaving him marooned here."

Carrying their snowshoes, the four strode through the deep snowdrifts towards the cabin. Darkness was coming on rapidly, and they moved like stealthy Indians, keeping a wary lookout for the intruder. However, they saw no sign of their enemy either on the way or near the cabin.

Cautiously Frank opened the door, entered, and lit the lamp. The place looked untouched. Everyone crowded in.

"Brr-r!" Chet shivered. "It's icy in here. Let's get a fire going."

Soon a cheerful blaze was crackling in the fireplace, and a woodstove fire added its warmth.

"Boy, that heat sure feels good," Chet said gratefully, rubbing his hands together over the potbellied stove. "Now for some chow!"

"Hold it!" Frank said. "We still haven't located Hanleigh. If he's not here in the cabin—"

"We don't know that for certain," Joe cut in. "There's one place we still haven't looked."

"Where?" Biff asked.

"The attic."

Frank snapped his fingers. "You're right—I forgot that. We'd better check."

"Give me a boost," Joe said, "and I'll soon find out."

Frank and Biff each took one of Joe's legs and hoisted him towards the ceiling. Pushing open the trap door, Joe clambered up into the attic and shone his flashlight all around through the chilly, musty darkness.

"How about it?" Frank called impatiently from below.

"No sign of him."

The others were uneasily silent as Joe lowered himself through the ceiling opening again and dropped to the floor, letting the trap door fall shut behind him.

Then Biff voiced what each boy was thinking. "Hanleigh's got to be somewhere on this island—unless he hiked back to the mainland."

"Well, there's only one way to make sure," said Joe.

Chet gave a groan. "Good grief! Don't tell me we have to go out and beat the bushes again. I'm starved!"

"Guess we all are," Frank said with a wry grin. "But I agree with Joe. If Hanleigh's skulking around the island anywhere, we'd better find him—and the sooner the better."

"Check! We sure don't want that creep coming back in the middle of the night to play any dirty tricks on us," Biff pointed out.

Chet's plump, ruddy cheeks turned a shade paler at the prospect of another night of ghostly episodes. "Okay, okay," he said hastily. "Let's get it over with."

Pulling on their heavy jackets again, the boys went

outdoors to make a thorough search. Flashlight beams probed behind trees and into clumps of bushes. An hour later they met inside the cabin, tired and cold. They had not found their quarry, nor any hiding place where he might take shelter overnight.

Frowning, Joe flung off his outdoor clothes and sat down cross-legged on the rug in front of the hearth.

"Hanleigh must have sneaked across the ice," he concluded, poking the fire.

Frank thrust his fists into his pockets. "I'm going to find out what that guy was doing here!" he declared.

"Well, I've had enough mystery for a while," Chet spoke up. "I'm starting dinner!" The plump boy headed for the kitchen. A moment later he came running back to the living-room. "It's gone!" he wailed.

"What's gone?" Frank asked.

"The food! There's not a bit left!"

"Hanleigh, I'll bet!" Biff declared angrily.

"Chet," Joe queried, "are you sure the food is not there?"

"Yes! Last night I put the boxes of grub we didn't use in the cupboards. You fellows saw me!"

For a moment the four hungry boys stared at one another in dismay. Then Frank said, "I can't believe Hanleigh came here to steal our food. Probably he hid the supplies just to inconvenience us so we'd leave. Let's check to see if they're stashed somewhere in the cabin."

The food could not be found. "We'll have to go to town for more groceries," Chet urged.

"It's too dark to take the *Seagull* out," Frank reminded him.

"We could always go home for supplies," said Chet.

"Not me!" exclaimed Joe. "No sirree!" He grinned wryly. "I can hear Aunt Gertrude saying, 'I told you so.'"

"We'd look like great detectives," his brother agreed, "when somebody can steal the food right out from under our noses."

"That's right," said Biff. "Besides, it's a long cold walk to the car."

"Oh, no!" Chet moaned as he sank down on the sofa, his hands on his ample stomach. "I'll starve!"

"Not for a month or two," Biff assured him.

"Hanleigh's mighty eager to have us give up this vacation," Joe said thoughtfully. "I wish we knew why."

"Of course we don't know for sure he did steal the food," Frank stated. "Maybe somebody else was here and took it."

"Well, at least we have proof Hanleigh was on the island while we were away," Joe reminded the others. "I'll get that photo!"

He opened the camera and removed the snap-shot. The young detective studied the picture, then gave a low whistle of surprise.

"What is it?" Frank asked as he, Chet, and Biff hurried over.

"Hanleigh's not alone!" Joe exclaimed.

The photograph showed him standing by the chimney, holding the stout stick with which he had been tapping and poking. Some distance behind him, partially hidden among the trees, was another figure. The stranger was dark and slim and was dressed in a long, flowing white robe. A turban covered his head!

·11·

A Cryptic Notation

"THE ghost that Chet saw!" Frank exclaimed as he stared at the snapshot of the white-robed man.

"Y-you think so?" Chet asked incredulously.

"It could be!" Joe declared. "I wonder who this person is, how he got here, and where he is now."

"Perhaps he came with Hanleigh," Biff suggested.

"I doubt it," Frank replied. "Look at the way the fellow's standing back in the shadow of the trees, almost as if he was spying on Hanleigh."

Frank paused, then added, "First thing tomorrow Joe and I will go to the mainland and phone Ike and Tad. If they're sore at Hanleigh, maybe they'll give us a lead on what his game is."

"Yes, and we'll ask if they're running a taxi service for a ghost!" Joe grinned.

"Maybe this turbaned fellow stole our food," Chet remarked. "Say, what are we going to do about that?"

Frank laughed. "Tomorrow Joe and I will buy supplies. But you and Biff will have to stay and guard the island."

"I'll admit I'm hungry as a bear, too," Joe said.

"Likewise!" Biff put in.

"Well, fellows," Chet began sheepishly, "I—er—forgot about this until now, but—er—we can have a snack."

The others stared at the rotund youth, who reddened as he explained. "When I made sandwiches for lunch, I put some away—in case of emergency!"

"Where are they?" asked Joe. "We searched all over this place!"

Chet went into the bedroom he and Biff shared and returned with five thick sandwiches in a large plastic bag.

"Come on! Where'd you hide them?" Biff asked.

"In the bottom of my sleeping bag."

"You weren't thinking of an emergency!" Joe scoffed. "This was to be your midnight snack!"

"Aren't you glad!" Chet countered.

"You win," Frank said, and they devoured the sandwiches.

Early the next morning Frank and Joe felt insistent fingers tapping them awake. "Get up!" Chet implored. "You have to go after groceries."

The Hardys dressed hurriedly. Frank told Biff and Chet, "While we're away, you might search the island for our stolen grub. Chances are that Hanleigh hid it all in one place not far from the cabin."

Frank and Joe set off in the ice-yacht, steered out of the cove, and soon were tying up at a nearby coastal summer resort named Surfside. The boys walked to the deserted main street. "Place is really hopping, isn't it?" Frank chuckled, surveying the tiny, weatherworn houses, many of them boarded up.

"Anyway, here's a phone." Joe pointed to an outside

booth. He stood by and listened while his brother dialled Ike Nash's number.

"No answer," Frank reported. "I'll try Tad."

The Carson boy was home, but his responses to Frank's queries were rude and unco-operative.

"I don't know anything," Tad insisted. "Hanleigh told us to scram and not to snoop around. So we left."

"How about a man wearing a white robe? Did you taxi him to Cabin Island too?"

"White robe? You're nuts!" Tad guffawed and hung up abruptly.

"That didn't accomplish much," Frank said wryly as he and Joe walked away from the booth. "Let's see if we can find a place to buy food."

Presently the boys stopped at a small wooden building. A sign above the door proclaimed:

GENERAL STORE, AMOS GRICE, PROP.

As the boys entered, a short, elderly man with a bald crown and skinny, wattled neck eyed them intently from his chair beside a black potbellied stove.

"And what might you lads be after?" he chirped.

"Hello," said Frank. "We're here for some groceries. Are you Mr Grice?"

"Yep. Odd to see strange faces around these parts here this time o' year," the storekeeper remarked.

"We're roughing it near here," Joe told the man.

Amos Grice clucked. "Most folks prefer sittin' by a fire when winter comes on. Well, you're out early this mornin'!"

"Necessity," Joe replied. "Somebody stole our supplies."

"I declare!" The old man looked startled. "Don't tell me there's more folks trekkin' about in all this cold and snow!"

"Seems that way." Joe grinned as he and Frank began to pick out canned goods and other food items.

"Where'd you boys say you're stayin'?" the store-keeper asked when the Hardys brought their purchases to the counter.

"On Cabin Island," Joe replied.

"Cabin Island!" Mr Grice repeated in surprise. "Has Elroy Jefferson sold the place?"

"No," Frank told him. "Mr Jefferson is letting us use his cabin during our Christmas vacation."

Frank paid the storekeeper, who then commented, "Elroy Jefferson's a fine sort. Haven't seen him in a while. What's he doin'?"

"He seems to keep busy travelling and collecting antiques," Joe replied.

Mr Grice propped his elbows on the counter and said thoughtfully, "Elroy Jefferson used to come in here every Tuesday for supplies, and the little fellow with him. He loved Johnny like his own son. And where's the youngster nowadays?"

"We don't know, Mr Grice," Frank answered, not wishing to reveal anything about their case to the friendly but gossipy proprietor.

"Mr Jefferson was always crazy about antiques," the storekeeper went on. "I recall how upset he was when his medal collection disappeared."

"Have you any idea what happened to it?" Joe asked.

"Nope. All I know is the medals disappeared and so

did John Sparewell, by some mighty big coincidence."

"Do people believe he stole the medals?" Frank asked.

"Not that I've heard. But it was odd he vanished at the same time."

The Hardys exchanged glances but did not comment, and Grice went on:

"You know, boys, just about a week ago a fellow was in here askin' about Jefferson's medals. I hadn't thought of 'em in years, before this fellow came by. Somehow I didn't feel right to tell him a thing, so I didn't."

"Who was this man?" Frank asked.

"Don't know. Never seen him before. He was a scary sort—dressed up like Halloween. He had somethin' wrapped around his head."

The Hardys' thoughts flew to the "ghost." Joe asked, "Do you remember anything else about the person? Did he tell you why he was interested in the medals?"

Amos Grice wrinkled his brow. "I got rid of that spooky fellow soon's I could."

After a few more minutes of conversation, the boys said goodbye and left. They walked quickly towards the *Seagull*.

"What do you think of Mr Grice's 'scary' visitor?" Joe asked his brother.

Frank replied, "I'm sure it was the man in the turban and the white robe. And he's apparently interested in the medals, too."

"Say!" Joe exclaimed. "Maybe he *is* in league with Hanleigh. I'll bet they're both after the collection and think there's some clue to it on the island."

The boys climbed into the *Seagull* with their bags of groceries. "I'll concentrate on your hunch while you take a turn at the tiller," Frank told Joe.

"Swell with me!" Joe grinned.

Out on the bay, the *Seagull* swerved and dipped like a live thing. "The wind's picked up!" Joe called out.

"I'll say!"

Joe deftly guided the ice-yacht towards the narrow inlet, the wind pushing them faster every moment. But suddenly it changed direction sharply. A wild gust whacked the *Seagull*'s sail. The craft tipped crazily and streaked straight for the rocky shore!

"Lean!" Joe shouted. The boys shifted their weight, and Joe threw all his strength against the tiller while Frank trimmed the sail. The boat began to turn, but the jagged rocks loomed close.

"We're going to hit!" yelled Joe, bracing himself for the splintering crash.

But the vessel skimmed past—safe by no more than two inches.

"Whew!" Frank said with a big sigh of relief.

Joe looked grim. "We're not out of trouble yet. This wind is tricky!"

Strong gusts continued to buffet the craft, but the boys were able to control it. At last the wind moderated and Joe steered their craft through the narrow inlet to the island.

When the *Seagull* was safe inside the boathouse, Chet and Biff came bounding through the snow to meet the Hardys.

"That was great sailing!" Biff exclaimed. "We were watching you."

"It was rough," Joe admitted, handing the groceries to Chet, who reached out eagerly for the bags. "I'm afraid the eggs are scrambled!"

"If they aren't now, they will be!" the cook replied, and headed straight for the kitchen. A short time later the four sat down to a delicious breakfast.

After the Hardys had reported on the trip to Surfside, Biff and Chet told of their failure to locate the stolen supplies.

"Let's look once more," Frank suggested, and explained that Tad and his pal knew nothing of Hanleigh's departure from the island.

"And he certainly didn't carry those heavy boxes across the ice!" Joe stated. All footprints had been obliterated by the wind-drifted snow, so their task was more difficult.

"Chances are they're hidden nearby," Frank said. "We'll go without snowshoes this time so we can kick up the drifts."

As soon as breakfast was over, they set out. First they searched in the snow which had piled against the cabin, but found nothing.

"Hanleigh probably carried the boxes out the back," said Frank, leading the way to the kitchen door. "Where is the nearest big drift?"

The boys looked around. Joe pointed to a mound of snow banked high against a large spruce at the edge of the clearing.

The four hurried over and began kicking into the drift. Suddenly Biff cried, "Ouch!"

"What's wrong?" asked Joe.

"Stubbed my toe on the tree!" Biff answered.

"Hey—no! It's a can of fruit!" He looked startled.

Chet dug eagerly into the snow and gave a whoop of joy. "Here's the chow!"

The boys carried the containers of food to the kitchen. "This time we unpack everything," Chet declared. "Then it won't be so easy for someone to cart off!"

As Frank helped to remove the contents, his hand came upon a small brown notebook lying askew between two cans of beans. He plucked it out.

"Look at this!"

"Whose is it?"

Frank thumbed through the damp pages, most of which were torn loose.

"Could this be the notebook we saw Hanleigh using?" asked Joe.

Frank examined a few more pages and gave a low whistle of surprise. "I doubt it. See here. The name on the inside cover is John Paul Sparewell!"

"Sparewell!" Joe exclaimed.

Biff shook his head, bewildered. "What was Sparewell doing here? Did he take our stuff? How many people are wandering around this island, anyway?"

Frank placed the notebook on the table where they all could examine it and began turning more pages.

"Wow! See this!" Biff exclaimed.

One of the loose pages contained a crudely drawn map. "That's Cabin Island!" the boys cried out in unison.

Another entry concerned rental of a boat.

"Whether or not Sparewell has been here recently,

it looks as though he was coming to Cabin Island regularly at one time," Joe remarked. "Just like Hanleigh is now!"

On a page near the back of the notebook, the boys found a list of receipts for small sums. "Sparewell evidently had very little money," Frank commented.

"He had problems, though," Joe observed. "Read the next item."

The scrawled script said, "Appointment with Dr Bordan on Sat. My condition worse. Would appeal to J but am afraid."

"I wonder if J is for Jefferson," Frank mused. "It sounds as though Sparewell was very ill. Perhaps he didn't live long after making these notes."

"I don't believe Sparewell was the one who dropped this notebook," Joe reasoned. "He'd have frozen to death over here." The boy frowned in perplexity as he turned to the last page. All four stared at it in astonishment.

"What kind of lingo is that?" Biff gulped.

The letters at the bottom of the page were:
HJOSW SHRJWN HLSEWPA RPAO A, EWO WSWP APPO LSUL

"A coded message!" Frank exclaimed.

·12·

An Ice-yacht Clue

"It's a coded message, all right!" Joe declared as the four boys continued to stare at the mysterious letters in the tattered notebook.

"How will we ever figure it out?" Chet asked.

"There are several methods of deciphering," Frank replied. "Dad has told Joe and me something about it, and we've read a few of his books on cryptography."

"Can you make anything out of this message?" Biff asked.

"Not right off," Frank replied. "It's some kind of substitution system, at any rate."

"The first thing to look for is transposition," Joe explained. "All the letters of the actual text—what's really meant—may be present, but reversed or scambled."

"There must be countless possibilities," remarked Biff, "once you start putting one letter in place of another."

"Yes, which makes deciphering very difficult," Frank agreed. "But I remember several of the standard patterns. I'll use some of the blank pages in the note-book and try them."

Frank worked for more than half an hour, while the

others looked on and made various combinations of the letters he jotted down.

"I'm stymied," Frank admitted finally.

Biff frowned. "How did Hanleigh get hold of this notebook? Does he know Sparewell?"

"Hanleigh might have swiped it," Joe said.

The Hardys pondered their next move. Joe suggested they take the ice-yacht model and the photo of the turbaned prowler to Mr Jefferson for possible identification.

"And on the way show Amos Grice the picture, too," Frank added.

A stop at the Hardy home also was included in the day's plans, in case the boys' father had any more information on the "alley" cat.

Chet heaved a huge sigh. "Which means Biff and I stand guard here."

Joe grinned. "How'd you guess?"

After a quick lunch the Hardys put on their parkas and boots. "I'm taking the camera along," Joe said. "It may come in handy again."

The Hardys climbed into the *Seagull* and headed for Surfside. At the dock, Joe tied up while Frank braked and slackened sail. Then they strode off to the general store.

Amos Grice, seated by the stove, slapped his knee when Frank and Joe walked in. "Glad to see you two. Thief steal your food again?"

"No, sir," Frank said. "We came to show you this." He handed the snapshot to Mr Grice. The storekeeper stared at it, then handed the picture back without comment.

"Mr Grice," Joe inquired, "is this the man who asked you about Mr Jefferson's medals?"

Amos Grice drew his lips into a thin, firm line.

"Yep. It's him. But there's some spooky business goin' on, and I don't want any part of it."

"Did this man say something to frighten you?" Joe persisted. "Did he threaten you?"

Mr Grice looked grim. "No. But I'm not mixin' in with any scary masqueraders."

The Hardys could see that the storekeeper would say no more on the subject. They thanked him and returned to the *Seagull*. A brisk wind sped them towards Bayport. They tied up outside their boathouse and drove home.

Mrs Hardy greeted her red-cheeked sons with big hugs, while Aunt Gertrude looked on apprehensively, as if trying to find something wrong with her nephews. Noting their excellent health, she turned her worries to their companions.

"Has something terrible happened to Chet or Biff?"

"No. Why, Aunty?" Joe asked.

"That sudden snowstorm. I was scared stiff for you boys. Some trees blew down over here."

Frank grinned. "We weathered it—howling banshee and all."

"A what?" Mrs Hardy asked, and her sons told of the whistling bottle.

"Well, I'm relieved to know that's all the trouble you ran into," Mrs Hardy said.

"Oh, there was more," Joe said. "By the way, where's Dad?"

"Out of town. But he left a message. It's in a sealed envelope on his desk."

Frank and Joe hastened to their father's study, found the envelope addressed to them, and tore it open. Inside was a terse note telling them that fingerprints found by the police in Mr Jefferson's ransacked house were those of Hanleigh. They had been identified by the FBI in Washington, where the federal agency had a record of interstate frauds involving Hanleigh several years before. The local police were looking for him.

"Aha! A con man. We might have known," mumbled Joe.

The message went on to warn the boys again to be cautious and ended, "Just as in fishing through the ice, you have to be patient. I'm confident that you'll land this big one."

Frank and Joe were more excited about the case than ever. With a quick "goodbye" to their mother and Aunt Gertrude, they hastened into their car and drove directly to Mr Jefferson's place.

"Frank and Joe!" the elderly gentleman exclaimed when he answered the doorbell. "Nice to see you! Let me take your jackets—my housekeeper is still away. Come right in. I hope you are enjoying your trip."

"We're having a fine vacation," said Frank as they took seats. "We wanted to ask you about a few things." Frank handed over the snapshot. "Have you ever seen this fellow?"

Mr Jefferson stared at it in perplexity. "What in the world!" he exclaimed. "I've never seen any such individual! Did you take this photograph on Cabin Island?"

"Yes, sir," Joe replied, and explained about the camera with the telescopic lens. The Hardys also told how they had observed Hanleigh examining the fireplace, and of overhearing Ike and Tad's conversation in the boathouse.

"The police informed me it was he who broke into my house," Mr Jefferson said indignantly. "The rascal! He should be punished."

The boys promised to do their utmost to apprehend him, and Frank told Mr Jefferson of finding the carved ice-yacht.

Their host's voice trembled with excitement. "Johnny used to make ice-yacht models!" he exclaimed.

"Oh, oh!" Joe said sheepishly. "Frank, I forgot to bring the model. It's still on the mantel."

"I must see it," Mr Jefferson said.

"Can you come to the island with us?" Frank asked.

"By all means!"

The three set off in the convertible for the boathouse. When he saw the *Seagull*, Mr Jefferson looked apprehensive. "I've never been in one of these contraptions. I understand they move rather swiftly."

"We'll put a rope seat belt on you and we'll be careful," Joe assured him. He gave the elderly gentleman a spare helmet and goggles from the boathouse, then helped him aboard.

After a few moments of uneasiness at the speed of the *Seagull* and the nearness of the ice which flew beneath them, Mr Jefferson appeared to relax and enjoy his ride. By the time they swept up to Cabin Island he was almost enthusiastic. "I never made better time in a motorboat!" He laughed.

When the three entered the cabin, Frank introduced Chet and Biff. Mr Jefferson took a long, slow look around the room, then spotted the carved vessel on the mantel. At once he hurried over to see it.

"Johnny made this!" he said with certainty, lifting the boat and running his fingers over its polished surface. "I'm convinced he did this carving recently. It's by far his finest."

"Did Johnny teach himself woodworking?" Chet asked in admiration.

"Yes," Mr Jefferson replied proudly. "The boy became intrigued with ice-yachts when he was very small. He used to spend hours watching them on the bay, and frequently went to the local boat shop to see how the crafts were made. Johnny would come home and carve until late at night."

Next, the Hardys showed Mr Jefferson the notebook containing the mysterious code and explained how they had found it. The man studied the book, shaking his head in amazement. "This is the first I've heard of Sparewell in two years!" he declared. "The cipher is a complete puzzle to me, but the book is exactly like him—methodical to the last detail."

"Why would Sparewell make a map of Cabin Island?" Frank queried.

"I can't imagine what interest he might have had in the island." With a sigh the old man pushed the book away. "I'm weary," he said. "I'd better return."

Once more the Hardys and Mr Jefferson set off in the *Seagull* towards Bayport.

Suddenly Joe shouted, "Look out!" Frank glanced about and saw another craft skimming straight for them. Its two occupants wore woollen face masks, giving them a grotesque appearance.

With swift teamwork the Hardys swung the *Seagull* out of the collision path.

"It's the *Hawk!*" Joe gasped.

Mr Jefferson gave a hoarse cry. "Here they come again!"

As the other vessel swooped alongside, one of the men lifted a short stout log from his lap and hurled it at the speeding *Seagull*.

Thud! It was a square hit on the bow. With a sickening swerve, the *Seagull* capsized. The temporary seat belts gave way. The Hardys and their passenger were flung across the ice!

·13·

The Fleeing Ghost

THE trio skidded across the glassy surface, with arms and legs flailing, until they came to a halt several yards from the overturned *Sea Gull*.

The Hardys had the breath knocked out of them but had suffered no injuries. Mr Jefferson, however, lay motionless. Greatly concerned, the boys jumped up and hurried to the elderly man's side.

"He's unconscious!" Frank said, and pointed to a swelling lump on Mr Jefferson's temple.

Joe ran to the *Seagull* and returned with a blanket, in which they quickly wrapped the man. Frank chafed his wrists until Mr Jefferson began to stir and moan. "We're going to crash!" he whispered.

"No, Mr Jefferson," Frank said in a reassuring tone. "The ice-yacht turned over, but we're all safe."

Their passenger raised his head and looked around. "Will you help me up, boys?" he asked. "I'm sure I haven't broken anything."

Carefully the brothers assisted him to stand. "Take it easy," Joe cautioned. "You had a bad spill."

"I'm all right. Just a bit shaky."

"We'll get you back to the cabin where it's warm just as fast as we can," Frank promised. "You're in no shape for a run to Bayport." He and Joe righted the *Seagull* and saw with relief that the mast was not damaged.

"The runner plank's a little out of alignment," Frank noted.

"That won't delay us," Joe said. "The bow's scraped too, but there's nothing we can't fix."

Frank eyed the improvised seat belts which had torn loose. "They couldn't take the strain," he remarked. The boys retied the ropes.

"That'll have to do for now," Joe said. "We were lucky this accident wasn't worse," he added as the boys helped Mr Jefferson into the cockpit.

"I'd like to report those ruffians," the elderly man fumed, "but we couldn't see their faces."

Frank said grimly, "We know the owners of the boat. They covered up the name, but I'd recognize the *Hawk* anywhere."

"That's no help, though," Joe added glumly. "We still can't *prove* Ike and Tad were the ones who attacked us."

In a few moments the *Seagull* was skimming towards Cabin Island. As they approached the boathouse, Joe suddenly pointed. "Frank!" he cried out. "Do you see what I see?"

"Yes! The ghost!"

The mysterious white-robed figure was halfway up to the cabin. It was proceeding stealthily through the bushes and pines that grew thickly on the incline. As Mr Jefferson stared ahead startled, Joe grasped the camera to which the telescopic lens was still attached. "I'm going to take another shot of that fellow."

His brother restrained him. "Wait! You'll only get his back. Let's sneak up close to him and see if we can get a face view."

"Good idea," Mr Jefferson said approvingly. "You boys go ahead. I'll wait in the boat."

A moment later the Hardys braked the craft and tied it to a tree alongside the boathouse. Silently they hurried up the wooded slope until they were a short distance behind the ghostlike figure.

A sudden idea struck Frank. He took out his police whistle and showed it to his brother. "Maybe this'll help us nab him," he whispered.

Joe nodded. "Got you." Cautiously the two advanced towards the prowler, who had now stopped and was peering out at the cabin from behind a tree. When the boys were a couple of yards away they paused also. Frank gave a signal, and as Joe raised the camera, blew a shrill blast on the whistle.

The "ghost" whirled about, and Joe snapped the picture. Frank blew several more blasts in rapid succession, and the robed figure bolted across the slope. At the same instant, Chet and Biff burst from the cabin and looked around wildly.

"Catch him!" Frank cried as he and Joe broke into a run.

All four boys bounded after the ghostly form, who darted nimbly in and out of the trees like a frightened deer. Dusk was beginning to fall and it was not long before the boys lost sight of the white robe against the snow.

They paused for breath, straining their eyes to pierce the gathering gloom. Then Frank barely made

Frank and Joe chased the ghostly figure.

out the fleeing figure at the bottom of the hill. The pursuers plunged downwards, but by the time they reached the spot, the "ghost" had vanished. There was not a sign of him on the ice.

Doggedly the boys continued to search along the shoreline, but had no luck. At last Joe said glumly, "No use going any farther. It's too dark to see."

Frank agreed. "We'd better get back and pick up Mr Jefferson."

On the way to the boathouse, the Hardys told Biff and Chet of the accident to the *Seagull*, deliberately caused by the *Hawk*.

Biff knotted his fists angrily. "I'd sure like to give those two guys a good stiff wallop."

"Of course we don't know for sure that they were Ike and Tad," Joe pointed out.

"Who else?" Chet groaned. "Some relaxing vacation this is!"

The young sleuths reached the *Seagull* and found Mr Jefferson waiting anxiously for news. "Afraid the 'ghost' escaped again, sir," Frank said regretfully, helping the old gentleman from the boat.

As the group walked slowly up the hill, Mr Jefferson shook his head, plainly disturbed. "Something very sinister is happening here. I certainly want to find out who is responsible, and what his motive is, but I do not want you boys getting into danger on my account."

"We'll keep on our guard," Joe assured him. "But we're all determined to see this mystery through."

"You can bet on that!" Biff declared stoutly.

Inside the cabin, Chet added logs to the fire as Joe eagerly took the picture from the self-developing camera. "Now we'll get a look at our ghost," he said.

The others crowded around and Joe held up the photograph of a young, dark-skinned man with startled eyes.

"Seems to be the same as the one in the first picture I took," Joe observed.

"At least we'll recognize his features if we spot him again," Frank said.

Mr Jefferson sank down on the sofa and sighed wearily. "I give up. This mystery is too much for me."

Frank urged him to rest for a while. The elderly man, smiling wanly, stretched out.

"You'd better plan to stay overnight, Mr Jefferson," Joe advised.

"I'd like to. I haven't spent a night on Cabin Island in years."

Meanwhile, Chet had gone into the kitchen and in a short time announced that supper was ready. Everyone did full justice to the hearty meal of fried chicken and hot biscuits. Afterward Frank offered their host the use of his sleeping bag.

"Thanks a lot, but I don't like to put you out."

"I insist, Mr Jefferson," Frank said. "We fellows will take turns standing guard tonight, anyhow, so only three of us will be sleeping at a time."

A nervous look crossed Chet's face. "And I can guess why! You're expecting another visit from that ghost!"

Biff could not resist needling his chunky pal. "Just think, Chet. You might even have the honour of nabbing him."

"Oh swell! I can hardly wait!" Chet rolled his eyes dramatically and the others laughed.

"Or," Joe remarked, growing serious, "Hanleigh may return for the notebook, if he's the person who lost it."

When Mr Jefferson had retired, Frank said, "Let's try to decipher the message!"

The boys sat down with pencils and paper. The Hardys told their friends more about solving substitution ciphers, and they all worked diligently for nearly two hours.

Finally Joe declared, "This code is a tough one. I've tried a number of combinations, but so far no luck."

Biff stretched and yawned. "My brain won't work any more. Let's get some sleep."

Joe offered to take the first watch, and Frank the second.

"I'll put in for last!" Chet requested wearily. Everyone laughed, and the plump boy protested. "Well, I've been doing all the hard work in the kitchen!"

Biff grinned. "Okay. I'm third."

"We'd better be ready for action," Frank advised. "Don't get undressed."

But hours later when Biff finished his watch, the place was still quiet. He awakened Chet, who wandered drowsily into the living-room. Yawning, he stared into the steadily burning fire.

"I have to keep alert!" he told himself with determination.

Chet began to pace around the room, trying to shake off his sleepiness. At last, when night was beginning to lift in the east, he sat down in a big soft chair near the fireplace.

The cabin's stillness and the warmth from the crackling logs was lulling. Chet's lids grew heavy, his head dropped, and he dozed.

Suddenly a loud *bang* jolted him awake. For a moment he was speechless, then a yell of fright burst from his lips. Before his chair hulked a dark figure!

· 14 ·

Chimney-top Discovery

As Chet shouted, the intruder streaked across the cabin and out the door, which was swinging wide open.

"Help! Fellows!" Chet bounced out of his chair, heart thumping with excitement, and dashed wildly in pursuit. But by the time he reached the doorway, the figure was already disappearing into the woods.

"What's up?" cried Frank as he burst into the room. Joe and Biff were close at his heels.

"Somebody was in here!" Chet said, shivering as the wind whipped into the cabin. "I drowsed off, and when I woke up, the guy was standing right in front of me! He ran down the hill!"

"It may be a ruse to get us out of the house," Frank said. He and Joe hastily pulled on their parkas and boots. "Chet, you and Biff stay on guard—he may try to circle back!"

Rushing outside, the Hardys quickly spotted the intruder's tracks—clear bootprints in the thin layer of fresh snow that had fallen during the night. They followed the trail down the wooded slope.

"He headed across the ice!" Joe exclaimed as they reached the shore. Pressing forward, the Hardy boys strained their eyes to peer through the grey dawn mist, but it was not light enough for them to see the fugitive.

"His tracks lead towards the mainland," Frank observed. "Come on!"

As the young sleuths crossed the frozen cove, they found that the snowy prints were more widely spaced.

"Oh, oh," said Joe. "He started running here."

When the brothers reached the mainland, breathing heavily, they exchanged looks of disappointment. The trail ended at a place where tyre prints showed a car had been parked.

"That fellow didn't waste any time!" Frank exclaimed in chagrin. "He must have had a big lead on us, or we'd have heard the motor."

"I guess we may as well go back," Joe said.

The two trudged across the ice. The sun was rising as they hiked up the slope to the cabin. Inside, a fire was blazing and Chet, Biff, and Mr Jefferson sat in front of it drinking hot cocoa.

"No luck," Joe said, and reported what they had found.

"Fellows, I'm sorry I let you down," Chet said sheepishly. "I dozed off and never knew the guy was in here until the door banged against the wall. He must have left it unlatched and the wind blew it open."

"That's okay, Chet," said Frank. "What did he look like?"

"I was too scared to notice, except that he was big. Besides, he was facing the fireplace. I don't think it was the ghost, though," Chet added, "because he didn't have on white."

"Could have been Hanleigh," Frank remarked.

"It must have been," Chet admitted.

"He still is interested in the fireplace," Frank observed.

"But why?" Mr Jefferson asked. "I built this place. Nothing's in the fireplace."

Frank hesitated, unwilling to raise the old gentleman's hopes. "That remains to be seen. Is there a chisel here?"

"Yes," Chet replied, "in the toolbox in the kitchen." He hastened out and returned at once with the tool.

Despite the heat, Frank stepped close to the fireplace with the chisel and pried at the stones, hoping to find one that moved. Meanwhile, Joe brought a ladder from the kitchen and climbed up to test the chimney rocks which Frank could not reach.

"No use," Joe finally admitted. "They're cemented in tight."

Frank agreed. "If there is a loose stone, it might be outside. Let's take a look!"

Chet cooked breakfast while the other boys were gone. The wind was blowing hard as the trio carried the ladder around the end of the cabin to the chimney.

"Let's check the bottom first," Frank said. This time Joe used the chisel as they poked and pushed at each of the large stones.

Biff shook his head. "No luck there."

"I'll go up on the roof and examine the chimney," Joe said.

Biff and Frank lifted the ladder and placed it beside the chimney. The legs sank into the snow and slid on the ice beneath, so that the boys had to brace the ladder with their feet to keep it from falling.

"You two'll have to be my anchor men," Joe said.

He put the chisel into his pocket, and as Biff and Frank leaned their weight against the ladder, he climbed to the roof. Joe crawled onto the edge and stood up gingerly. The heat from the fire below had melted the surrounding snow and the wet shingles were slippery. Joe made his way around the chimney, testing each stone patiently with his chisel, but none was loose.

As he rested a moment Joe noticed a fragment of yellow material caught between two stones just inside the chimney top.

Squinting against the smoke, Joe reached in and worked the material loose. With watering eyes, he stuffed it into his pocket and turned his face away. After a few moments his vision cleared and he could see the entire island below—blanketed in white.

Suddenly his glance was caught by a dark patch ringed by tall rocks on the brow of the cliff. As he stared hard at it, the wind suddenly cut sharp across his face and showered him with snow from the roof. Half-blinded, he felt his way around the chimney to the ladder.

"Be careful!" Frank called, but the wind whipped the words away. The next moment Joe slipped and he fell with a cry. Instinctively he grabbed for a rung and caught it. The ladder skidded at the jolt and the boys below struggled to hold it steady. Shakily Joe climbed down.

"Thanks," he gasped, reaching the ground.

Buffeted by the wind, the three boys made their way into the cabin.

"Any luck?" Mr Jefferson asked as they took off their parkas.

"I found this inside the chimney," said Joe, and took the piece of yellow material from his pocket.

"It's a piece of a tape measure!" Frank exclaimed. "See, it's marked one inch."

"It was stuck tight," Joe said. "Someone must have torn the tape trying to pull it loose."

"But why measure the inside of the chimney?" Chet asked.

"Maybe the person thinks the loose stone is in the chimney lining," Mr Jefferson suggested.

"You mean there are two layers?" Biff asked, surprised.

"Yes. My stone mason insisted on a lined chimney as a safety measure." Then he added, "What makes you so sure there is something hidden in the chimney?"

"We're not certain," Frank confessed. "We suspect it because of Hanleigh's interest in the fireplace. But for all we know, he may be on the wrong track."

"We must crack the code," Joe declared. "That will probably give us the answer."

"Not before breakfast," Chet said firmly. "I'm about to make the pancakes." He hurried to the kitchen and a short time later served stacks of golden-brown cakes, with a pitcher of hot maple syrup and a platter of spicy sausages.

"Chet, you've redeemed yourself!" Joe exclaimed, between mouthfuls. "This hits the spot after our early-morning exercise!"

Mr Jefferson was quiet during most of the meal. Finally he said, "Do you know? It has just occurred to me that Sparewell mentioned a relative named Hanleigh."

Frank asked eagerly, "What did he say about him?"

"It was so long ago—I can't remember," Mr Jefferson replied.

"That may be an important clue!" Joe exclaimed. "Perhaps Johnny stumbled onto the connection somehow and decided to start trailing Hanleigh."

"Yes," Frank went on, "if Johnny was determined to solve the puzzle of your missing medals, he may have dug up information about Sparewell's past and learned the names of relatives. Then, when Hanleigh showed up at your home, Johnny had his chance to follow him."

"It's all supposition," Mr Jefferson said with a sigh. "What we need are facts."

"Well, speaking of facts," said Joe, "are there hot springs on this island, Mr Jefferson?"

The man looked at him in amazement. "Hot springs! Certainly not! My goodness, Joe, whatever made you ask that?"

"Oh," Joe mumbled vaguely, "nothing—just an idea." But his eyes met Frank's and the older boy bit back a grin.

"Nothing, my foot!" he said to himself. "Joe's found a clue!"

· 15 ·

The Shah's Prize

"WHAT can Joe's lead be?" Frank wondered. He knew his brother was not ready to talk about it in front of the others.

Frank turned to Mr Jefferson, who seemed sunk in despair. "Don't give up hope," the boy said kindly. "We'll keep trying to find Johnny and your medals, too."

"If anyone can locate 'em, the Hardys can," Chet put in.

"I know that. You're all fine lads, and will do your best," Mr Jefferson said, brightening somewhat. "I think I'd better return home now."

"Are you sure you feel strong enough, sir?" Biff asked anxiously.

"Yes, indeed," the man assured him. "I'm warm now, too. And if you don't mind, I'll take along this carved model. It will give me reassurance that Johnny will come home."

"Certainly, Mr Jefferson," Frank said, taking the yacht from the mantle.

"And Sparewell's notebook," Mr Jefferson added suddenly. "It may contain clues for my detectives."

Frank spoke up. "We'd like to keep the notebook a

115

little longer. Joe and I want to study it carefully and crack that code."

Mr Jefferson nodded. "Of course. You've certainly earned the right to examine it first. But please be careful, boys. Possession of the notebook may be dangerous, if someone else wants it badly enough."

Joe offered to stand guard on the island while the others accompanied Mr Jefferson to the mainland.

A short time later the *Seagull* went whizzing out of the cove, with Frank at the tiller. They made a quick trip to the Hardys' boathouse, then drove to the Jefferson home.

As Frank parked the convertible, Chet suddenly gave a gasp of disbelief. He pointed a quivering finger at the wide front porch and cried out, "It's—it's the ghost!"

Frank leaped from the car, with Chet and Biff close behind him and Mr Jefferson following slowly.

The white-robed, turbaned figure darted away from the door as the boys dashed up the front path. He jumped off the far end of the porch and disappeared around the side of the house. The three youths sprinted in pursuit, but soon stopped short, scanning the landscape. Their eyes roved over the snow-covered walks and flower beds, the birdbaths capped with ice, and the bare bushes and trees. The "ghost" could not be seen.

"That white robe is great camouflage against the snow," Biff commented glumly.

"Let's split up and search!" Frank directed quickly.

The boys hunted while Mr Jefferson stood and watched in tense silence. Suddenly Frank noticed a blur of whiteness moving behind a hedge of low junipers.

The young sleuth stepped backwards, took a running start, and vaulted the shrubs. A loud cry split the air as he landed on top of a crouching figure. The two rolled over, struggling.

"Hold 'im, Frank!" yelled Biff. He and Chet sprinted up and yanked the slender, white-robed man to his feet. The boys gasped as they got a clear look at the prisoner's dark-skinned, frightened face. No doubt about it, he was the man in the photo!

"Okay, Mister Ghost—what's your story?" Biff blurted angrily. "You have a lot of explaining to do."

"Take it easy," Frank told his friend. "Let's get him inside first."

Panting, the captive was led into the house.

"Now then," said Mr Jefferson when they had all gathered in the living room, "who are you? And why have you been prowling on my property?"

The swarthy man replied in a soft, slightly accented voice, "I apologize for my seeming intrusions. I ran because I was startled, and also these young men have pursued me previously. The last time one of them was carrying a firearm."

The Hardys grinned and Frank said, "My brother Joe was holding a camera with a telescopic lens. From a distance it does resemble a rifle."

"Ah," said the man, "I see." He smiled faintly. "I am seeking Mr Elroy Jefferson."

"I am he," said Mr Jefferson. "Just what is it you want?"

The stranger now stood up and took an official-looking

red-and-gold diplomatic passport from inside his robe. With a slight bow, he showed it to Mr Jefferson.

"I am Yussef ben Karim. I represent the ruler of my country—our great Shah Ali. I understand that among your valuable medals is one that was given many years ago to the Shah's grandfather. This medal is most prized by my master and he has authorized me to pay whatever sum is required to obtain it."

Mr Jefferson shook his head. "I'm sorry to say that I don't have your medal. I once owned it, but unfortunately my collection was stolen. I'm still searching for it."

Yussef looked bewildered. "But I was given to understand that Mr Hanleigh would have the medal for me."

The boys and Mr Jefferson exchanged startled looks. "What do you mean?" Mr Jefferson asked.

"Mr Hanleigh sent word to the Shah last summer saying that you had appointed him to act as your agent, and I was instructed to meet him here, which I did. You, sir, were not at home. Mr Hanleigh first told me that he had the medal, but later he declared it was not in his hands—that he would have it soon. I beg you, what is the truth?"

"That's what we're trying to find out," Frank interjected. "Yussef, that man Hanleigh was lying to you. For one thing, I'm quite sure he had no right to pose as Mr Jefferson's agent—"

"He most certainly did not," the elderly man stated emphatically as Frank turned to him for confirmation. "Hanleigh is the last man in the world whom I would entrust with such a matter, even if I still had the medals and wished to sell them."

"What's more," Frank added, "Hanleigh probably doesn't have the medals, either, and never did have them."

Yussef's face registered concern. "I was afraid of that. The Shah will be grievously angered."

Frank told Yussef that the boys were working on the mystery, and added, "My theory is that Hanleigh's scheme in contacting the Shah was to set up channels through which he could sell the medals—if he found them—without being prosecuted. We suspect Hanleigh had been searching for the collection on Cabin Island."

"Tell me, Yussef," Biff put in, "what were *you* doing on the island?"

The man said apologetically, "I am sorry. I did not intend to trespass. I had begun to suspect Mr Hanleigh's story about the medal, and followed him there on two occasions. Like you, I could not escape the impression that he was seeking something hidden and wondered if it might be the Shah's medal."

"And you looked for it yourself?" Frank asked.

"That is correct. But I had no success, and finally I deemed it wise to come directly to Mr Jefferson."

"How did you get to Cabin Island?" Chet asked.

"But of course, I walked," Yussef replied with a smile. "I overheard Mr Hanleigh talking with the two young men whom I have seen transporting him to the island in an ice-going craft."

"Now you understand the whole situation, Yussef," said Mr Jefferson. "I agree with my young detective friends that Mr Hanleigh evidently hopes to locate the medals for his own gain—including the one desired by your ruler."

"It is a great misfortune to have lost so fine a treasure," Yussef declared sympathetically, "and to be persecuted by an unscrupulous person such as Mr Hanleigh."

"At least we won't be off chasing ghosts!" Chet added a little sheepishly. "When I first saw you, I thought you were a spook!"

The foreign visitor laughed along with the others, then Frank said, "We'd better get back to the island and see how Joe's making out."

Yussef's expression became sombre. Gravely he said to Frank, "If your brother is alone there, you must hurry to him. I have a feeling he is in danger. Mr Hanleigh can be violent."

"We know it," said Frank. "We'll leave right away."

Meanwhile, Joe had left the cabin with the binoculars and was trudging towards the cliff, eager to test the theory that had been forming in his mind.

As he stepped from the shelter of the woods, the sunlight was dazzling on the snowy ground which led to the cliff edge. Beyond lay the frozen bay.

Joe's eyes sought the circle of tall stones he had seen from the roof. They stood near the edge of the cliff about fifty yards to his right. With a surge of excitement, he strode towards them. "Now—" he said to himself, "we'll see!"

Suddenly Joe stopped. Below, an ice-yacht was skimming across the inlet. He swung his binoculars up and trained them on the craft. Joe stiffened.

"The *Hawk!*" he muttered. "Ike, Tad, and Hanleigh!"

Quickly Joe made his way downhill and hid in a clump of bushes near the dock. He watched as the craft was guided ashore and tied up. The three paused close enough for Joe to hear Hanleigh say:

"You punks keep an eye out for the Hardys and their pals. Give a shout if you see anyone coming." Then the man started towards the cabin.

Joe waited until Ike and Tad had walked off down the shore, then returned noiselessly up the slope. Cautiously he peered into the living-room of the cabin— no one was there. Joe hurried to the rear and crouched among some bushes below the window of the Hardys' bedroom. He raised his head and peered in.

Hanleigh was rummaging through the brothers' belongings! "Bet he's looking for the notebook," Joe thought. "Good thing Frank has it with him."

Suddenly Hanleigh spun round and Joe ducked. He heard the man's outraged bellow. "Spying again, are you!"

· 16 ·

The Intruder's Revenge

"How did Hanleigh spot me?" Joe thought desperately, crouched low amidst the bushes. Moments later, the kitchen door opened and footsteps scrunched towards him on the snow.

To Joe's surprised relief, the big man strode past his hiding place and disappeared around the side of the cabin. Before Joe could move, Hanleigh's angry voice rang out.

"Couldn't resist snooping, could you?" he snarled. "I haven't paid you two just for the taxi services—I've been paying you to mind your own business."

Ike Nash and Tad Carson!

Joe smiled wryly. "They must have been looking through that little end window in my bedroom."

Ike's whining voice came to his ears. "We were freezing! There's a fierce wind off the ice."

"That's a real shame!" Hanleigh retorted. "You fellows come with me. I'll show you a place to keep warm!"

The three rounded the corner and Joe held his breath as they plodded past him. He poked his head from the bushes in time to see Hanleigh open the woodshed. "Wait in there!" he ordered.

Unsuspecting, the two roughnecks stepped inside. Hanleigh pushed the door shut and bolted it. "I'll take good care of the *Hawk* for you!" he sang out tauntingly.

From within the shed came angry yells as Ike and Tad pounded violently on the door. Chortling, Hanleigh turned towards the kitchen.

"Let us out of here!" Ike screamed.

"You don't know how to run the yacht!" Tad cried frantically.

"Oh, stop your chatter!" Hanleigh shouted. "I won't wreck it! Do you think I'd take a chance with my own skin?"

Again the two prisoners pounded and kicked at the door. "You got no right to hold us!" Ike yelled. Hanleigh paid no attention.

Joe came to a sudden decision. "I must hold Hanleigh here until the others get back!"

The young sleuth stood up resolutely and called out, "So you're trespassing again, Mr Hanleigh!"

The man gave a start. Upon seeing Joe, his face contorted in rage. "You meddling spy!" he shouted. "I'm not trespassing. I came after my own property! Get out of my way!"

Joe walked up to Hanleigh and asked calmly, "Did you lose a notebook? One that has John Sparewell's name inside?"

Again Hanleigh started guiltily. "I don't know anything about a notebook," he replied sullenly. "I came for my wallet. I lost it last time I was here. You probably found it, and you'd better turn it over or I'll have the law on you!"

"Did the message in code tell you to come looking for something valuable on Cabin Island?" Joe persisted.

Hanleigh swung his fist. Joe ducked and butted the man hard in the chest. With a grunt Hanleigh staggered back against the cabin.

"You're a scrapper, eh?" he panted.

"Anything you start, I'll finish," Joe said. He watched the man warily, but Hanleigh only gave an ugly smile. "I'll fix you later," he said softly. "No use hanging around now."

He turned and plunged down the hill. Joe followed, keeping an eye on him. At the dock Hanleigh untied the *Hawk* and sped for the inlet.

"Too bad I couldn't hold him here," Joe thought. Then he remembered Ike and Tad in the woodshed, and grinned. "But I still have his buddies!"

He headed quickly up the hill towards the cliff. At the top Joe looked down, but could see no sign of the *Hawk*. "Hanleigh made good time," he said to himself, then the young detective's thoughts returned to the cluster of stones he wanted to investigate.

When Joe reached the spot, he quickly circled the tall rocks and spotted a narrow opening between two of them. He stepped through and found himself on a small patch of rocky ground, damp with melted snow. He knelt and felt the stones. They were warm! From several crevices arose wisps of smoke.

"Somebody has built a fire below," he murmured. "Clever! Nobody'd ever notice the smoke."

The thin streams drifting to the top disappeared in the wind.

The next moment Joe heard a noise and a soft laugh behind him. For an instant he froze. *Hanleigh!* Too late the boy flung himself sideways. A hard blow landed on the back of his head. He sank into darkness!

When Joe regained consciousness, he was first aware of the intense cold and of a throbbing sensation in the back of his head. His aching eyes saw a low roof of snow above him. Then he realized his wrists and ankles were tightly bound.

"Hanleigh!" Joe thought. "Where is he?"

The big man was nowhere in sight. Joe struggled to free himself, but every movement tightened the stout cords.

"Boy, what a mess!" Joe muttered in disgust. "I'll just have to wait until Frank and the others come back." He noticed that his feet and hands were growing numb, but managed to wiggle his toes and fingers. "I'll have a swell case of frostbite if they don't show up soon."

At that moment Frank, Chet, and Biff were streaking towards the inlet in the *Seagull.* Suddenly Chet pointed. "Look!"

Out of the narrow channel sped an ice-yacht with a lone occupant at the tiller.

"Hanleigh!" Frank exclaimed. "I wonder what happened to Ike and Tad!" A chill went through him. "And what about Joe?"

"Let's go after Hanleigh!" Biff cried out.

Frank shook his head. "We should get to the island pronto. Something's fishy about this whole business. Joe may be in danger."

In a short time their craft was tied up, and the three boys hurried straight up the slope to the cabin.

Frank threw open the door. "Joe!" he called anxiously. "Hey, Joe!"

There was no answer.

"Listen!" Chet exclaimed. Loud bangings and scufflings could be heard.

"Joe might be locked in the attic!" Biff said. They all rushed into the kitchen, then paused in confusion.

"Not the attic," Frank said. "Those sounds are coming from the woodshed!"

The others followed as he dashed outside and unbolted the door of the lean-to. "Joe—" he began, then stopped abruptly as Ike and Tad half stumbled into the open.

"What are you two doing here?" Biff demanded in amazement.

"Where's Joe?" Chet asked.

"Joe?" Tad snapped. "Where's Hanleigh? And the *Hawk?*"

"Yeah!" Ike put in. "That guy's a dirty double-crosser. He tricked us into this icebox and locked us up."

"Right now Hanleigh's taking off in your boat," Frank told them, then added sternly, "Never mind about him. What happened to my brother?"

"Don't look at us—we never saw him!" Tad replied. "We thought you were all away from the island."

"After Hanleigh trapped us in that shed, we don't know what he did," Ike added, whining. "We just kept banging and yelling."

"Maybe you'll be more careful what kind of people you take up with after this," Chet said. "And think twice about causing boat accidents, too."

"Aw, cut the lecture, fatso," Ike sneered.

Frank turned to Biff and Chet. "I'm going to find Joe. Something's happened to him. You take those two inside, and don't let them go. I want to question them later."

"You think Joe is in danger?" Chet asked fearfully.

Frank looked worried. "I'm afraid so. It's a big island," he added grimly. "I hope we're not too late."

· 17 ·

The Dangerous Climb

"Joe!" Frank called repeatedly as he slowly circled the island searching for his brother. The young sleuth had nearly reached the cliff when his shouts were answered by a faint cry.

"Here! Over here!" Then silence.

Frank thought the sounds had come from a clump of tangled underbrush and hastened to it. Pulling aside the snowy branches, he saw Joe. The blond boy was so numb that he could barely move his lips. Quickly Frank untied the cords on his brother's ankles and wrists.

"Think you can walk?"

"I'll try," came the faint reply.

Joe leaned heavily on his brother and the pair made their way haltingly towards the cabin. When they drew near, Frank shouted, "Biff! Hurry!"

The muscular youth came sprinting outside and together he and Frank carried Joe into the living-room and placed him on the sofa. Chet, heaving a sigh of relief, rushed to get a blanket.

After a few minutes, Joe felt stronger. Presently he drank a cup of hot cocoa, then said, "I'm okay."

Just then he noticed Ike and Tad, standing glumly

next to the fireplace. Joe grinned. "Did you have a nice warm wait in the woodshed, fellows?" As they scowled, Joe told his story without mentioning why he had gone to the cliff or what he had found there.

When Joe had finished, Biff strode over angrily to Ike and Tad. "What's Hanleigh after on Cabin Island?"

"That's what we wanted to find out," Ike answered. "Say, won't you guys give us a lift to Bayport so we can find the *Hawk*?"

"Are you kidding?" Chet retorted scornfully. "You expect a ride in the Hardys' ice-bus after you tried twice to wreck it?"

"How did Hanleigh find out we were going to stay on Cabin Island?" Joe queried.

"We were picking him up down the road when he spotted you packing the *Seagull*," Tad explained. "Hanleigh eavesdropped on you near the boathouse and heard your plans."

"We've just been doing his dirty work," Ike said sourly.

"You could have injured someone seriously throwing that log at the *Seagull*," Frank said. "Mr Jefferson was knocked out."

"Don't blame me. I wasn't there!" Ike whined.

"It's true," Tad admitted. "Hanleigh and I wore masks. It was his idea to disable your boat."

"But how could you be sure we would be coming out in the *Seagull* at that time?" Joe asked.

"We were on our way to the island when we saw you," Tad replied. "Hanleigh changed his mind about the trip and decided to ram you. He made me take him ashore to pick up a log. Then we lay in wait near the inlet. We didn't realize you had the old man until too late."

Despite further intensive questioning, Ike and Tad stuck to their statement that they knew nothing of Hanleigh's quest on Cabin Island, nor had they seen a boy answering Johnny Jefferson's description. Finally the troublemakers departed, grumbling, to walk home.

As soon as the door had closed behind them, Joe swung off the couch. "Fellows," he said, "I've something to tell you."

"And about time!" exclaimed Frank. "I've been burning with curiosity. Why did you ask Mr Jefferson about the hot springs?"

"And what were you doing on the cliff?" Chet put in.

Joe interrupted. "Take it easy. Let me explain. I think I know where Johnny Jefferson is."

"Where?" chorused the others.

"In a cave in the cliff."

"How do you figure that?" Biff asked.

Joe told about spotting the patch of dark ground from the cabin roof. "At first I figured there was a hot spring melting the snow. Later it occurred to me that, instead, there might be a cave under the spot. If someone built a fire in it and there were crevices in the roof leading to the surface, the smoke would come up and the heat would melt the snow."

Frank's eyes flashed with excitement. "Great deduction, Joe!"

"I got only as far as the circle of stones," Joe went on. "Smoke was coming up, so I'm sure somebody was in the cave—probably Johnny. But Hanleigh knocked me out even before I could look for the entrance."

"Then he dragged you to a place where you could freeze waiting to be rescued," Biff put in grimly.

"The mouth of the cave is probably in the cliff face!" Frank declared. He jumped up and started pulling on his parka. "Come on! We'll surprise Johnny and bring him back here!"

"Wait!" exclaimed Chet. "First lunch!"

After a quick snack, the boys headed for the cliff. On the way, Frank told his brother about the meeting with Yussef.

Joe whistled. "Hanleigh's a sharp operator, all right. I wish I could've made him admit he was after the medals. He was plenty upset when he found out we had the book and the coded message. I'm sure he hasn't solved the cipher yet," Joe added.

When the boys reached open ground at the top of the cliff, they were met by an icy blast from the bay. Frank glanced anxiously at the leaden sky.

"Storm coming," he muttered.

Joe showed them the sheltered spot in the circle of stones. No smoke was rising.

"The fire must have gone out," Frank commented.

"Since the cave is right under here," said Chet, "the way down may be nearby."

"Let's look for footprints leading to the edge of the cliff," Biff suggested.

"It won't be much use," Frank said, shaking his head. "This wind will have swept them away."

The boys walked to the rim and looked down at the jumble of ice-coated crags which jutted out, hiding the sheer wall below.

Biff shivered. "One slip and goodbye, Charlie!"

"Maybe we'd better forget about it," Chet said hopefully.

"No," Frank answered. "If Johnny Jefferson can get down there, so can we. But we need our climbing boots and flashlights."

"I'll go back and get them," Chet volunteered quickly, and started towards the cabin.

"Hurry!" Frank called after him. "It'll be dark soon."

"It's dark in here already," Chet muttered as he entered the woods. He ploughed along the trail the boys had made earlier, wishing he had not come alone. The white woods was eerie and the pines moaned and tossed in the wind, showering him with snow.

Once Chet put up an arm to protect his face and stumbled off the trail into a clump of brush. He fought clear, found the path again, and went on.

Suddenly the wind stopped. Startled by the silence, Chet paused.

Why did he feel he was not alone?

As he stood, breathing heavily, he heard a low moan behind him. It rose into a weird cry and trailed off into silence.

Chet's lips opened and closed, but he made no sound. With effort he forced himself to look back. Was there something tall and white standing against a snowy bush? As he strained to see, the thing vanished among the trees. With a hoarse cry Chet plunged down the trail and did not stop until he was in the cabin. Gasping, he locked the door and leaned against it.

"Can't be sure I saw anything," he had to admit, a

little ashamed. "But I heard that weird cry, I know."

The thought of his companions waiting on the cold cliff top forced Chet to gather up the boots and flashlights and go out again. By the time he came to the end of the woods, he was red-faced from running.

"Over here!" Frank called, and Chet hastened along the cliff top to where his friends were waiting.

"Fellows," he burst out, "there's another ghost here! I saw it in the woods!"

Joe grinned and took the equipment from his plump friend. "Great joke, Chet, but we've heard it before."

"I'm not kidding! It gave a terrible—"

"We've no time to waste," Frank broke in, hanging a flashlight on his belt. "Get your gear on." Grumbling, Chet obeyed.

"We think this is the best place to start down," Frank told him.

He walked to a crevice in the cliff edge about six feet deep, and lowered himself to the bottom. From there he stepped on to a flat icy ledge, digging in hard. Beyond it stood another jutting stone. Frank moved ahead, and, one by one, the others followed him on rough footholds across the cliff.

Occasionally they stopped and examined the rocky wall for an opening, but saw none. Once Chet glanced towards the inlet and froze at the sight of the drop.

"Don't look down!" Joe shouted.

Frank, making his way along a ledge, stopped to look back at his companions. Just behind him was a narrow opening between the cliff and a slab of rock which angled out from it. About twenty feet above, Frank could see the circle of stones.

"This may be the cave!" he thought, and signalled to the others.

As they stood in a line on the ledge, he indicated the opening and gestured for silence. Then Frank led the way into a dark passage which opened into a rock chamber, dimly lit by a pile of glowing embers.

"Nobody here!" exclaimed Joe, his voice sounding hollow.

Against one wall was a stack of cans, food boxes, and pots. Nearby lay a sleeping bag, a box of tumbled clothes, and an unlit paraffin lamp.

"This is the hideout, all right," Frank said. "We'll settle down and wait for Johnny."

"It might take a long time," Biff remarked.

"I doubt it," said Frank. "With a storm coming up, he's probably heading for here right now."

For a while the boys sat in silence, then suddenly they tensed. A footstep in the passage!

As they scrambled to their feet, Biff stumbled over the lantern. It turned over and clattered across the stone floor. Instantly the footsteps in the passage stopped, then hurried away.

"After him!" Frank cried out. "Johnny!" he called. "Come back! We're friends!"

As the boys emerged from the passage they were met by roaring wind and swirling snow. Frank shouted again, but the words were lost. Daylight was nearly gone. The boys peered back across the cliff, but there was no sign of anyone.

Anxiously the Hardys looked upwards. Had the boy tried to climb to the crags above the cave mouth?

"No one there!" said Joe.

"Chet! Don't look down!" Joe shouted.

"Don't see him here or anywhere!" shouted Biff.

With sinking hearts the four looked around the cliff, each with the same unspoken fear.

Chet suggested, "Maybe he's hiding behind a rock."

"Let's hope so," Frank thought grimly, then said aloud, "No one could survive a storm on this cliff. If Johnny's hurt or hiding, we must find him."

It was decided that Joe and Biff would examine the cliff from above. Frank and Chet clambered down towards the ledge. Now and then they stopped and shouted, and looked for a figure among the crags. But Johnny was not in sight nor did he reply.

When they reached the jutting rocks at the ledge, the boys lay down and peered over the edge. With a gasp Frank pointed. Something white lay among the jagged rocks at the base of the cliff.

"A wreck!" Chet said. "An ice-yacht!"

"And there's somebody in it!" exclaimed Frank.

· 13 ·

The Crash

"SOMEBODY'S hurt!" said Frank. "Come on! Let's get Joe and Biff."

He and Chet climbed to the top of the cliff, where their companions were waiting.

"Any sign of Johnny?" Joe asked anxiously.

Frank shook his head and breathlessly told about the wrecked ice-yacht.

"We'll find the nearest spot we can to climb down," said Joe.

Frank took the lead. The foursome, their flashlights turned on, plodded through the deepening dusk and wind-whipped snow. Finally Frank stopped at the far end of the cliff, where the terrain sloped more gently. "I think we can make it here."

The descent seemed interminable, since the boys had to wind their way round boulders, high drifts, and in and out of thickly growing pines. At last they reached the shore and stepped onto the ice. Facing into the screaming wind, they headed towards the wrecked boat.

As the boys drew near the scene, Joe shone his beam on the tilted hull and yelled, "It's the *Hawk!*"

"Who's the man?" Biff called as the others rushed up.

"Hanleigh!" Frank exclaimed with surprise.

As the Hardys and their friends carefully freed the man, he regained consciousness. Groaning loudly, he clutched his right leg. It did not appear broken, so the Hardys helped him to his feet. Hanleigh took a few steps, then insisted he was in too much pain to walk.

"I think it's just a wrenched muscle," Frank muttered to Joe. "But give me a hand and we'll carry him."

Making a chair of their hands, Frank and Joe transported their heavy burden to the cabin, where they settled him on the sofa. Hanleigh grimaced with pain as Biff pulled off his boot. "I know my leg is broken," he complained bitterly. "And I nearly froze to death out there!"

"You had no qualms about leaving Joe to freeze in the snow this afternoon," Frank said.

Hanleigh's only response was a prolonged groan.

"Why'd you take the *Hawk* out in this storm?" Joe asked. "You must have been desperate to pay us another visit! And in a stolen boat at that."

"I only borrowed that old boat," Hanleigh growled.

"We know that isn't true," Frank retorted.

Hanleigh raised his head to glare at the boys. "Cut it out!" he snarled. "Can't you see I'm in terrible pain? You'd better get me to a doctor fast!"

"That's out of the question," Frank said, "until the storm lets up."

The boys exchanged uneasy glances. They realized that the violence of the storm also made it impossible to search for Johnny Jefferson.

"Hanleigh," Joe said sharply, "it's high time you

levelled with us. Have you seen Johnny Jefferson on this island?"

"I don't know what you're talking about."

Frank described the boy. "Now what about it? Have you seen him?"

"No," barked Hanleigh. "I've seen nobody, but—" He broke off and looked uneasy.

"But ghosts?" Joe asked with a grin.

"You think it's funny? You'll find out!"

"We've already caught the spook in the attic," said Biff. "It was the wind blowing over a lemonade bottle."

At the look of astonishment on Hanleigh's face, the boys laughed. "Let me alone!" he burst out. "I don't want to talk."

He would say no more, but ate greedily of the hearty supper which Chet prepared. He maintained a stubborn silence, refusing to answer further questions put to him by the young sleuths.

The Hardys learned nothing from him about his interest in the fireplace or his meetings with Yussef. The boys noticed, however, that his eyes travelled frequently to the chimney.

Finally the injured man fell into a deep sleep. "At least he can't escape," Joe remarked. "Too bad we can't get some information out of him."

"There's one thing we can do," Frank said in a low tone. "Break that code."

The boys hurried into the kitchen, and Joe closed the door. They settled down at the table with pencil and paper, the notebook turned open to the page bearing the cryptic letters. Soon all four became oblivious to the storm's increasing fury as they concentrated on the task.

Suddenly Frank exclaimed, "I think the first and second words are 'Cabin Island'!"

"How can you tell?" Chet asked.

"The number of letters are the same," Frank pointed to the HJOSW and SHRJWN of the code.

"Look. The words *cabin* and *island* both contain A, I, and N. So, the letter J stands for A, S for I, and W is N."

"Terrific!" Joe exclaimed. "Then, H is C, O is B, R equals L, and N stands for D."

"Let's try to find the key," said Frank. "I'll set up the alphabet." The others watched intently as he wrote:

ABCDEFGHIJKLMNOPQRSTUVWXYZ
JOHN   S   R   W   H

"*John Sparewell!*" Joe burst out. "But what does H stand for?"

"Houseman, maybe," Frank replied. "Try that. There's a comma in the cipher," he added. "It may stand for R."

"John Paul Sparewell, Houseman," Joe read. "That's the key. Now substitute those letters for the ones in the code."

Frank printed rapidly and held up the result:

HJOSW SHRJWN HLSEWPA RPAO
CABIN ISLAND CHIMNEY LEFT
A, EWO WSWP APPO LSUL
FRONT NINE FEET HIGH

"We've got it!" Joe shouted exultantly.

"But," said Biff, "we've gone over all the chimney stones."

"Remember, there's an inner lining," Frank pointed out. "As soon as the fire dies down, we'll check."

"You think Hanleigh deciphered the code?" Chet asked.

"No," Frank replied. "Otherwise he wouldn't have been so eager to recover the notebook."

"I'd still like to know how he got his hands on it," said Biff. "Did he steal it from John Sparewell?"

"I don't know," Joe replied, "but I vote we zero in on the medals pronto."

The boys' discussion was broken off by a signal for silence from Frank, who pointed to the door.

From the other side came the sound of creaking of floorboards. Swiftly the Hardys scooped up the notebook and the papers and hid them in a cupboard. Then Frank and Joe went over and pushed open the door a crack.

They peered out and saw Hanleigh limping to the fireplace. He pulled aside the guard from the fire, now burning low, took a poker and thrust it up inside the chimney.

"Bet he was eavesdropping," Joe muttered.

"Well, the code directions won't do him much good without tools," said Frank, and stepped into the living room.

"Looking for something, Mr Hanleigh? Glad to see your leg is better."

The big blond man wheeled, his face purple with

rage. "I'm sick of being hounded by you pests. I'll fix you—"

Hanleigh lunged forward, brandishing the poker, but tripped on a rug and went sprawling. The poker flew from his hands. Quickly Frank retrieved it.

"I wouldn't try that again," Joe said in warning tones as Chet and Biff rushed in.

Scowling, Hanleigh dragged himself over to the sofa and sank down heavily. "All right, all right. I was just going to stir up the fire," he mumbled. "It's cold as an iceberg in here."

The boys had to agree, because the wind had risen to great velocity and gusts shook the cabin. Icy draughts seeped beneath the outside door and the windows were half covered by driving snow.

"Maybe I'd better stoke the fire," Chet said.

Joe nudged him. "Later. We have something to do first."

Chet grinned. "That's right. Well, I can turn out a snack, anyway. That'll warm us."

The stout boy headed for the kitchen, but the next instant stopped in his tracks as a shrieking blast of wind struck the front window full force.

With a loud crash the entire pane shattered inwards. The freezing wind roared inside, knocking over all the oil lamps. Fire flared along the spilled fuel and Joe leaped forward, flailing at the flames with his parka.

Hanleigh rolled off the couch as his terror-stricken voice shrilled through the darkness. "Get me out of here! The whole place is going to collapse. I'll be killed!"

· 19 ·

A Frightened Thief

"QUICK! Into the kitchen!" Frank ordered. "Grab the parkas!" Hanleigh limped out hastily and the others followed. Having smothered the flames, Joe entered last and locked the door.

Their prisoner sprawled onto a chair and listened apprehensively to the roaring wind. "I never heard anything so bad before. What're we going to do?"

"Stick it out," Frank replied coolly. He eyed the rattling window over the sink. "We'd better board that up," he said, "and the ones in the bedrooms, too. Come on! We can rip up some of this flooring."

Chet brought two hammers, some nails, and a crowbar from the toolbox. For half an hour the sound of ripping boards and hammering could be heard through the noise of the storm.

As the four boys worked, they saw that the snow had drifted almost to the tops of the windows. Their thoughts went again to Johnny Jefferson.

Frank visualized the boy lying injured behind a crag on the icy cliff. "Joe," he said quietly, "as soon as the wind lets up we must go looking for him again."

His brother nodded. "I know."

When everyone gathered in the kitchen once more,

Chet said, "I think we'd better fill the wood box and bring in some extra logs. If the drifts get any higher, we won't be able to open the back door."

He put on his parka, took a flashlight, and plunged outside.

Suddenly there was loud pounding on the door. Joe looked surprised. "What's he doing back so soon?"

Biff opened the door and Chet fairly fell inside.

"The ghost!" he gasped. "In the woodshed!" The boys stared at their trembling chum in amazement.

"I guess he's not kidding," said Frank. "There's something out there. Come on, Joe!"

The Hardys stepped out and trudged through Chet's tracks to the woodshed.

Frank pulled the door open and flashed his light inside. Cowering in the corner was a white turbaned figure!

"Yussef!" Joe exclaimed.

But a moment later he saw that he was mistaken, as Frank pulled the white-robed figure of a young boy to his feet. *Johnny Jefferson!*

The Hardys knew him instantly from the photograph Mr Jefferson had given them. But he was more sturdy and better looking than they had imagined.

"Good grief!" Joe exclaimed. "What are you doing here?"

"Quick, into the cabin!" Frank commanded.

Wordlessly, the boy stumbled ahead of them towards the kitchen. Biff, Chet, and Hanleigh looked up in astonishment as the trio entered.

"Here's your ghost, Chet," said Joe. "Johnny Jefferson. That's right, isn't it?"

Johnny nodded, a frightened look on his face.

Chet found his voice. "You must be frozen, Johnny. I'll get some soup."

"Thanks." The boy removed the turban and the white robe. Underneath he wore a heavy jacket, ski pants, and climbing boots.

"Who are you?" he asked the boys, then nodded toward Hanleigh, "Friends of his?"

"Certainly not," said Frank. He introduced everyone and explained why they were on the island.

Johnny looked at them anxiously for a moment, then said, "Okay. I'll buy that."

"Good. Mr Jefferson sure will be relieved to hear you're okay," Frank said.

Then Johnny turned to Hanleigh. "You lied to me," he burst out. "You promised to teach me to be a detective, so I could find my grandfather's medals. But I know now you wanted them for yourself."

Hanleigh pretended he was not listening.

"Sit down and eat, Johnny," said Chet, serving a steaming bowl of soup. "Cheese sandwiches coming up."

The lad broke into a smile. "Gee, thanks." He began eating hungrily. "I thought you fellows were working with Hanleigh," he said, between bites. "So I decided to play ghost and scare you off. I got the idea from somebody else in a white robe and turban who was prowling around here and scared Chet." He glanced at Chet. "I'm sorry. That howl in the woods really shook you!"

As Chet grinned, Johnny could not repress a chuckle. "The trick worked so well that I decided to scare

Hanleigh, but I couldn't find him. When I got back to my cave I heard a noise inside, so I ran away."

"Where did you hide?" Frank asked.

"In a crevice I knew about in the rocks above the passage. Later I saw you hunting for me, but I kept out of sight."

"Suppose you start from the beginning," Frank said. "How did you get mixed up with Hanleigh?"

"Well, one day last summer when Gramp was in Europe, Hanleigh came to the house to see him about buying Cabin Island. Our housekeeper sent Hanleigh away, but some loose pages fell out of a notebook he was carrying."

"And you found them?" Frank asked.

"That's right. There was a map of this island and a plan of the cabin. Next time he came to the house I gave him the papers he had lost. I questioned him, too."

Hanleigh looked up. "I thought he knew something about the value of the medals so I kidded him along. Turned out he didn't know anything."

After a few more bites Johnny continued:

"At first I believed Mr Hanleigh was a detective and when I got back to school I wrote to him several times, but he didn't answer. I began to suspect that he was trying to find the medals for himself. About two weeks before Christmas I ran away from school and came to Cabin Island to see if Hanleigh was here. I hoped I could find Gramp's medals myself."

"He's worried about you," Frank said. "You should have seen his face when we gave him that model you carved. We found it by the boathouse."

Johnny looked concerned. "I didn't mean to worry Gramp. I'm glad he liked the carving. I carved it to pass time in the cave. I wondered where I'd lost it."

"You've been living in that cave all this time?" Chet asked.

"No. At first I lived here in the cabin, but when Hanleigh started coming around, I moved out fast. I had a key and came back for a couple of blankets." As to the cave, Johnny said he had played in it for years, but had kept its location a secret.

"What about the letter from Texas you wrote your grandfather?" Joe asked.

Johnny smiled. "I read about that trick in a detective story. I sent the letter to a friend of mine in Texas and asked him to mail it—and not to tell anyone. I was afraid Gramp might suspect I was here at Cabin Island and would send his detectives after me."

As Johnny finished, the wind suddenly shrieked and a strong draught made the oil lamp flicker. Hanleigh turned pale.

"If this keeps up," Frank said, "we'll have to dig our way out. It's going to be rough."

"But I can't do that!" Hanleigh exclaimed. "I'm hurt! And I'll die if you leave me here alone!"

Joe looked disgusted. "We'd send somebody back for you, of course."

Hanleigh's eyes filled with suspicion. "No you won't. Why should you? What's in it for you?"

As Biff was about to retort, Frank winked at him and shook his head. "I'll tell you what's in it for us, Hanleigh," he said, assuming a hard tone.

"Information! You tell us your whole story and I promise you'll be rescued."

The man looked up in relief. "Now you're talking my language. It's a deal. Here!" With trembling fingers he pulled a long envelope from his pocket and shoved it across the table. "Read this."

Frank reached into the envelope and took out a document and a letter. He scanned the document first.

"Good grief! This is John Sparewell's last will and testament!" Frank exclaimed. "Hanleigh is his nephew and sole heir."

"Sparewell dead!" Johnny said sadly. "When did that happen?"

"Last spring," Hanleigh volunteered. "Now read the letter from my uncle's lawyer."

Frank did so. "This letter," he told his companions, "which is dated last April, explains that Sparewell stole the medal collection when he was pressed for funds. Then he realized that no dealer would touch it."

Hanleigh interrupted. "Uncle John never tried to find a private outlet for the medals, the way I did."

"On his deathbed," Frank went on, "he requested that his nephew return the collection to Mr Jefferson."

"Why didn't he do it himself, earlier?" Chet asked Hanleigh.

"Because he was chicken, that's why. Uncle John was afraid old man Jefferson would try to bring him to justice. He wanted the medals to be in an absolutely secret place, so he thought of this cabin. On one of Jefferson's trips my uncle spent a weekend hiding the collection out here in the chimney lining. But at the time he didn't tell me where," Hanleigh complained.

"The next I heard about the collection was when he died and I came into possession of the notebook with a clue to this island and the secret code."

"Was it part of your tape measure we found in the chimney?" Frank asked.

Hanleigh nodded. "I guessed the medals were in there or the fireplace, but I couldn't crack the code."

"We know it was you who ransacked Mr Jefferson's house at Christmas," Joe said. "You're wanted by the Bayport police."

"I was a fool!" Hanleigh confessed. "I thought maybe the old man had found the medals and was keeping them in the house."

"After you stole our food," Biff said, "where did you go? We scoured the island for you."

"I walked back to the mainland road and hitched a lift to Bayport. Those two young punks with the ice-yacht ran out on me."

"I guess it was you who came in here the other night," Chet spoke up. "You knew we were here. Why did you risk it?"

"I had a feeling you were getting close to where the treasure was hidden," Hanleigh replied. "I wanted to find out if you were searching the chimney, and also to retrieve the notebook. It's rightfully mine. I figured you'd all be asleep."

Johnny sighed. Joe flung a quizzical look at the boy. "What's the matter?"

"We still haven't solved the main part of the mystery. Nobody knows for sure where the medals are." Johnny added wistfully, "And I did so want to find them for Gramp."

Joe grinned. "I've got news for you, Johnny—we've cracked the code."

As the boy exclaimed in delight, Hanleigh groaned and put his head on the table.

"As soon as the storm dies down, we'll start hunting," Frank said. "If the collection is here, we'll find it."

They remained in the kitchen for warmth and managed to snatch a couple of hours' sleep. The rest of the night passed fitfully.

Shortly after daybreak, Frank awoke and stretched his aching muscles. Noticing that the wind had abated, he opened the door to the big room. Things were topsy-turvy and under a blanket of snow. "The fireplace of the chimney first," he thought. Returning to the kitchen, he awakened the others. "Rise and shine, fellows! We have some treasure hunting to do, remember?"

After a quick breakfast, Frank said, "Joe—Biff, how about giving me a boost up the fireplace chimney?"

Frank turned on his flashlight and started to crawl into the fireplace.

At that moment the front door burst open. Two men stepped in.

"Hold it!" said a sharp voice. "You're under arrest! All of you!"

·20·

The Hazardous Search

WHIRLING in astonishment, the boys saw two stern-faced harbour policemen striding towards them through the debris in the living-room.

The Hardys recognized them as Lieutenant Daley and Officer Thorne.

"We're taking you all into custody!" barked Daley. "Where's the stolen ice-yacht?"

At that moment Hanleigh appeared at the kitchen door. "What's going on?" he asked, then gasped at the sight of the policemen. Despite his injured leg, he bolted for the back door.

Frank and Joe dashed forward and seized him. "Here's your thief, Lieutenant Daley," Joe said as they hustled the big man into the living-room.

The officer stared, astonished, upon recognizing the brothers. "The Hardys!" Daley exclaimed. "Didn't know you at first. You all look a little beat up."

Joe introduced the others. "We've been roughing it and trying to solve a couple of mysteries."

"They solved them, too," Chet put in proudly.

Johnny Jefferson stepped forward. "That's true," he said. "Frank and Joe and their pals have been working on a case for my grandfather, Elroy Jefferson."

"Then you must be Johnny Jefferson!" Lieutenant Daley exclaimed.

"Yes, the Hardys found me."

"Well, I'll be a frozen rookie!" Officer Thorne burst out. "We've been on the lookout for you!"

"Leave it to the Hardys," said Daley, tilting back his hat and scratching his head. "A couple of chips off the old block. How's your dad?"

"Fine," Frank replied, then told their story which included the wrecking of the *Hawk*. Handcuffs were snapped on Hanleigh.

"You can't take me to jail," he argued. "I'm a sick man."

"You'll be taken care of," Daley said firmly.

"By the way," Joe spoke up, "who accused us of stealing the ice-yacht?"

Lieutenant Daley explained that an anonymous phone call to headquarters had reported the theft, and revealed that the culprits were hiding on Cabin Island.

"Ike or Tad made that call, no doubt," Frank said.

Biff grinned. "Those two would be burned up if they knew they'd done us a favour tipping off the police."

Chet gave a wry chuckle. "Those guys will have a real surprise when they see the *Hawk*."

Daley added, "We didn't want to bother Mr Jefferson until we found out what was going on here, so we came straight over."

Hanleigh declared he was unable to walk. The police were unsympathetic. "You seemed to manage okay when you were trying to get away," Daley said. "So you certainly can hike across the cove to where our squad car is parked."

The lieutenant smiled at Johnny. "We'll tell your grandfather you're safe and in good hands."

Johnny pleaded that he himself wished to surprise his grandfather. "Besides, I want to take him his medals. I know the Hardys can find them."

"We'll give it a good try," Frank promised.

The two policemen agreed to keep the secret, and left with their prisoner, who complained bitterly as he was escorted from the cabin.

Without further delay the boys gathered round the hearth. "Now for the rosewood box!" exclaimed Joe, and went for a metal tape measure he had seen in the toolbox.

"What do you look for first?" Biff asked.

"A loose stone, nine feet up the front," Frank replied. He ducked into the soot-blackened fireplace and stood up. "Lucky it's a wide chimney," he remarked, picking up his flashlight. "Well, here goes. Give me a boost, somebody."

Biff crouched down in the fireplace and Frank sat astride his broad shoulders. Slowly Biff stood up, grasping his friend's legs. Frank unwound the tape, and with the aid of his flashlight, found the nine-foot level. He marked this off with chalk and handed the tape to Biff.

Then Frank began testing the stones in order from right to left. All felt tightly in place, but suddenly Frank touched a joint of cement which crumbled beneath his fingers.

"This looks much lighter in colour," he observed, "as if too much sand was used in the mix."

"Any luck?" came Joe's eager voice from below.

"Not yet. But I've come across something I want to investigate."

"Need help?"

"You can hold this light."

Joe squirmed in beside Biff and took the flashlight from his brother. Frank drew out his penknife and inserted the blade tip into the cement, which surrounded a large oblong stone. The substance fell off readily. Frank then grasped the rock and pulled hard. It gave a little.

"Hey!" exclaimed Joe. "What's cooking?"

"I'm not sure," Frank replied, "but I've just dug out some cement I think was mixed by an amateur."

"Sparewell?"

"Yes. He must have cemented the back of this rock, though. I need a lever."

"Hold on. I'll get something."

Joe hurried to bring the chisel. Frank placed it beneath the rock and worked the tool up and down. Finally the big stone moved. Now Frank used the chisel on both sides, prying the rock loose still more. Again he pulled hard on it. This time the stone came out in his hands. Quickly he gave it to Joe, who beamed the light upwards into the space. Frank saw that his guess had been correct! Working carefully, he succeeded in extracting a long, flat box.

"I've found it!" he gasped.

Frank scrambled down from Biff's shoulders and the trio emerged from the fireplace with sooty grins of triumph. Breathless, Frank flipped open the catch and raised the lid. Set in velvet was an array of handsome, gleaming medals!

For a moment all the boys stared at the treasure, then Chet exclaimed, "Wow! They're real beauties!"

Biff pounded the Hardys on the back while Johnny burst out, "Frank and Joe, you're the world's greatest detectives!"

His face shining with joy, he urged that they return to Bayport immediately. "I can't wait to give the medals to Gramp."

"We ought to clean up some of this damage before we go," Frank said.

"Chet and I will take care of that," Biff volunteered. "We'll board up the broken window and sweep out the snow and debris."

Frank grinned. "Okay, then. As soon as Joe and I wash this chimney dirt off and change clothes, we'll hit the road."

"I wish we could whiz home in your ice-yacht," Johnny said, "but it's impossible with all that snow."

"We'll come back for the *Seagull* when the ice is clear," said Joe. "You can ride in it then."

In a short time the Hardys were trudging across the cove with Johnny between them, clutching the rosewood box.

On the main road they hitched a ride to the Hardy boathouse. The trio were just about to climb into the convertible when Joe spotted a familiar car pulling into the parking area.

"It's Dad!" he exclaimed. The boys hurried to meet Mr Hardy.

The investigator smiled broadly upon being introduced to Johnny Jefferson and learning of the successful outcome of the Cabin Island mystery. "Great work!"

he praised his sons, and added, "I'll confess I've been uneasy ever since I sent that message and left you the note at home. So when I returned today I decided to go to the island, even if I had to hike!"

"You were right, Dad, about Hanleigh. He was out to get us," Frank declared. "Where did you learn about him?"

"I asked Chief Collig to brief me on the Christmas night break-in at Mr Jefferson's," Mr Hardy explained. "Shortly after you boys had left on your camping trip, the fingerprint report came back. So I hurried to the dock here, hoping one of your friends would give me a lift.

"Just then I saw an ice-yacht put in by our boathouse. I recognized the Nash and Carson boys aboard and soon realized the big blond man with them was Hanleigh. They were talking loudly about you and made some pretty nasty threats. They were gone before I could nab Hanleigh myself."

"So you sent Mack Malone to warn us!" Joe said.

"Right," his father replied. He had alerted Chief Collig and the Bayport squad had been on the lookout for Hanleigh. "He was a crafty customer with that ice-yacht," Mr Hardy said, "and gave everybody the slip until you fellows nailed him."

The famous detective also told the boys that just before leaving home he had received directly from Collig word of Hanleigh's arrest. The prisoner had made a formal confession—to taking the *Hawk*, breaking into Mr Jefferson's house, and scheming to steal the medals. "He also admitted the attack on Joe," Mr Hardy concluded.

"What about Ike and Tad?" Frank asked solemnly.

"They won't be charged as accomplices, since they did not know what Hanleigh was up to," Mr Hardy replied.

"But twice those two tried to wreck our boat," Joe said hotly. "And they accused us of stealing the *Hawk!*"

"I know," said Mr Hardy. "But both say they were only joking. Don't worry," the detective added with a grin, "Chief Collig gave them a stiff lecture. They won't dare get out of line for a long time."

Frank smiled. "Anyway, they'll be too busy repairing their ice-yacht to make any more trouble."

A short time later the Hardys and Johnny stood at the front door of the Jefferson home.

As Frank reached towards the doorbell, Johnny cried out, "Wait! I—I can't go in! Gramp will be angry!"

"No, he'll be happy to see you," Frank reassured the younger boy. "Besides, you have a surprise for him, remember?"

Johnny gazed at the rosewood box he held tightly and smiled. "You're right."

Frank rang the bell. When Mr Jefferson answered, he stared at his grandson incredulously. "Johnny!" The old man's voice rang with joy.

The Hardys stood by beaming as they witnessed the happy reunion. It was not until they were seated that Mr Jefferson became aware of the box Johnny carried.

Mr Jefferson was so overcome with emotion that it was several moments before he could speak. He turned to Frank and Joe.

"How has all this happened?" he asked, taking the box and opening the lid.

As the young sleuths and Johnny rapidly recited the amazing events, Mr Jefferson sat back in the crimson velvet chair, stroking the medals and looking affectionately at Johnny. "Wait until my detectives hear of your success, Frank and Joe. They'll be thunderstruck!"

Johnny said admiringly, "I'd sure like to learn from the Hardys how to solve mysteries!"

Mr Jefferson eyed his grandson proudly. "I underestimated you, son. You can take care of yourself."

Johnny beamed, then said worriedly, "You should see the cabin, Gramp. The storm did a lot of damage."

"No matter," replied the old man. "We'll start repairs and improvements this spring." He turned to the Hardys. "I want you both to feel free to stay on the island any time you wish to. Johnny and I are going there as soon as possible together—that is, if he'll take me along when he gets his new ice-yacht."

"Gramp! Do you mean it?"

"Indeed I do! Since my ride in the *Seagull*, I've been looking forward to another spin on the ice."

Frank and Joe exchanged smiles. Mr Jefferson was not so old-fashioned after all! Their sleuthing had done something to change his attitude. The young detectives did not know that events were already occurring which would soon involve them in another challenging case, *The Mark on the Door*.

Mr Jefferson added, "I intend to present the Shah's medal to Yussef. But first—" He lifted two handsome pieces from the box and said to the Hardys, "I wish to give you each a remembrance, in gratitude."

"Thank you, sir, but we can't accept," Frank protested. "They're too valuable."

"Besides, we've had our reward returning Johnny and the medals to you," Joe added.

Mr Jefferson smilingly insisted, "These are rightfully yours. Remember, their purpose is to reward exceptional merit and courage. No one ever earned them more than you Hardy boys!"